POLITICIANS

ARE SUPERHEROES

by Peter Clarke

POLITICIANS ARE SUPERHEROES

Copyright © 2018 by Peter Clarke

Cover: Mark Dwyer
Layout and Design: Pski's Porch

ISBN-13: 978-1-948920-01-8
ISBN-10: 1948920018

for more books, visit Pski's Porch:
www.pskisporch.com

Printed in U.S.A.

1.

On the seven o'clock news, that familiar jingle and the intro that sucks you in and gets you excited for what's to come:

POLITICIANS ARE SUPERHEROES.

Let them do a running contest to prove it. Then let's see how they lift tall buildings. Pluck the moon out of the sky and throw it at the sun. Take that, sun!

When crime shoots off the charts they have SPEECHES. When bridges crumble at the knees they have ALIBIS. When the economy free falls into the gutter they have EXIT STRATEGIES, CLEVER DISGUISES, and ALTERNATE CAREERS LINED UP IN LOBBYING.

They've got the legislative process and plenty of red blood. Also they've got your VOTES!

Remember the politician who saved the planet from being sucked into a black hole? He just hooked up with the foreign diplomat who solved the Middle East problem. HOT SHIT!

Want a good time? Check out the live reenactment of how the earliest superheroes invented alcohol on the same day they built a temple to the sun. Then they got drunk!

Get your t-shirts on sale now with politicians' slogans including all of your favorites: "Champions Are Beautiful!" "Huge Muscles Will Set You Free!" "Eat the Crybabies!" "Don't Mess with Everything I Do Is Awesome!"

Where do they come from? That's the great mystery! What are they going to do next? Let's FIND OUT!

2.

Two monarchs sat in an old western saloon. One of them, Charlie, had been retired for the past six hundred years. Over that time, he'd put on nearly as many pounds in beer weight. His drinking partner, Al, had also been recently pulled out of retirement and was depressed.

Slumped over on his bar stool, Al held his crown in his lap. He twirled the crown around and around like a sad, sideways Ferris wheel. Which jewel should he pluck? One of them had to go.

Finally he found one. It was both small and illusive. It wouldn't be missed.

Al reached to pluck it. But it wasn't a jewel at all—only a drop of sweat fallen from his forehead.

"Let me see that," said Charlie, grabbing the crown from Al's lap. "Here's a perfect little sacrifice! The next round of drinks is coming right up!" He pinched a mid-sized diamond between his fingernails and pulled. He pulled and pulled. Pinched again, and kept pulling. But no luck.

"Let me get that fer ya, pardner," said the bartender, ready with a pair of pliers. A moment later, POP!

Al took his crown back and placed it on his bald, sweaty dome.

"Cheers, Al!" said Charlie, raising a fresh pint.

Al didn't bother to raise his glass. Gulping down the lukewarm suds, he stared up at Charlie's crown. It stared back like a grinning mouth of pulled teeth.

3.

Robbie Cox was doing one-arm pull ups when the election results came in. All around, his family and friends burst into tears and shouts; they jumped up and down and embraced; they streamed confetti and drenched the room in a shower of champagne.

After one more pull up, Robbie hopped down and spread his arms out wide to give the whole world a big group hug. Amazingly, everyone fit. People in the Arctic took off their coats, feeling suddenly warm inside. Beaches everywhere were instantaneously mobbed with people overcome with the urge to strip and go for a swim. In war zones, fighters on both sides set their weapons down and raised their hands over their heads, fists clenched, triumphant.

Robbie Cox also raised his hands over his head, fists clenched. The group hug was over. He kissed his bicep muscles. The power of victory was upon him. It was time to take that power and conquer his enemies.

4.

This chapter was supposed to be about an alternate political state. It's called Dudebuddy Nation? But we haven't been able to locate the files on it, so...

Supposedly there were ten boxes of files laying around here just the other day. Dug up from some ancient, cursed burial grounds. That's according to the head editor, anyway. But what are we supposed to do about that? We're just the copyeditors. If they want to hire a service for finding missing (stolen?) ancient documents, by all means!

Here's the gist, according to the legends we've heard:

There's an island nation of a free people that's totally apolitical. There's no politics whatsoever. Not sure if that implies there are no superheroes? Or maybe everyone there is a superhero?

In Dudebuddy Nation, all you do is party all the time. An ancient treaty makes it the case that the governments of the cosmos won't interfere with any of their business. So what's there to do but party? That's the idea, anyway.

Note that the "island" may not be a literal landmass in the ocean. Instead, the term "island" may be in reference to a sort of parallel universe. Or another planet, maybe? Then again, the legends generally do refer to palm trees, sandy beaches, and scantily-clad babes, so who knows.

Anyway, that's basically what the kids learn about in their unauthorized comic books—usually the self-published type. Sure wish we had kept our hands on some of those back in the day! But that's another story.

5.

POP QUIZ

1. Who was the first president to save the world from machines taking over?

2. What famous politician first saved everyone from the super bug?

3. Who led the Battle of Epsilon Eridani?

4. _____ was the president who won with 100% of the votes.

5. BONUS: Who's my favorite politician?

6.

Schools don't teach politics. Bottom line. No politics at school. There can be rare exceptions, sure. It's not like politics is porn, exactly. It's not like there's no place for politics in school. No, it's just that it's not needed. Keep that stuff out on the playground, if you're going to bring it to school.

It's almost all that kids ever seem to care about. Do they

want math problems? No way! How about some music lessons, some astronomy, or some time in gym class? Nope, not if they have a choice! All they want is politics.

All day long, it's superhero politician this and superhero politician that. It's enough to drive an educator bananas.

But every now and then, when the kids have been extra scholarly, they can get a little treat of politics in the classroom. A pop quiz all about politics, for example. Whoever gets the most right gets a poster of the president lifting weights!

7.

Recess time, Ms. Buckingham let everyone go except Killian Gladstone. At eleven years old, Killian hadn't yet learned how to approach a teacher with confidence. It would be a long road ahead before he learned how to take criticism like a champ. But he made it to her desk without breaking into a sweat, so that was a start.

"Killian, I'd like to talk about your answers on the quiz," she said.

"My quiz?"

"Yes. Who was the first president to save the world from machines taking over? The correct answer is Harold Rickenbaum. You wrote…Dudebuddy. And that's what you wrote for all your answers." Ms. Buckingham almost said the name again, but she stopped herself, wincing at the thought. "Did someone tell you to write that, Killian?"

"No," said Killian, looking down at his shoes.

"It's okay, you can tell me the truth. Who told you to write that?"

"Nobody."

"So you wrote that yourself? It was your idea to write that?"

"I guess so."

Ms. Buckingham sat back in her chair. Her demeanor changed. Her sympathetic features turned sharp.

"Killian, I'm going to have to tell your parents about this. I don't know how you ever heard of a name like that before. You must know it's not acceptable in this classroom. I'll let your parents handle it from here, but I don't ever want to see that name written down again, do you understand?"

"Okay!" said Killian, suddenly red in the face as if angry. "Fine! But, well, why don't you shut up about politics then, huh?!"

Killian reached up and nabbed the quiz out of his teacher's hands and bolted.

8.

Owning politicians is big business, especially if you're in the comic book or movie business. Some people own lots and lots of minor politicians—mayors, city council members, maybe a state senator or two. Other people invest bigtime in one of the goliaths in politics. If you own the secretary of state and a few legislators on the World Senate, you're set to be reeling in the profits. Throw in a president and a high class foreign diplomat or two and you're sitting pretty for life.

Not too many people know much about that. But Eleanor George does. She's the owner of a long list of Who's Who in the superhero pantheon.

Eleanor George. The media tycoon, the cultural icon, the legendary phantom limb yanking strings on political activities everywhere.

9.

INTERNATIONAL NEWS AND POLITICS REPORT: Eleanor George has purchased Robbie Cox with a record-setting bid. Details coming soon!

10.

Uncle Jon did science for a living. Science in terms of boiling different colors of liquids in different shapes of vials, wearing big plastic goggles when pouring one liquid into another, crashing into the laboratory's back wall after an explosion of toxic chemicals, and emerging from a haze of purple smoke with a maniacal grin of having once again answered some ultra-subtle mystery.

If Uncle Jon were a political slogan on a campaign hat, it would be: "Lab Rats for Explosives!" If he were a political slogan on a button, it would be something clever involving the periodic table. If he were a political slogan on a beer-stained t-shirt, it would be: "Get Your Arse Ready for Eureka!" with a cartoon of Archimedes jumping up from a bath sporting an arse extra plump.

Uncle Jon wasn't a politician. He wanted to be, but he was born lacking in superpowers. His arms were weak, his legs were gangly, his capacity for public speaking was nil, etc.

Long after hours, Uncle Jon would sneak into the lab of the mega corp where he worked. He'd help himself to the extra fancy equipment and the extra dangerous chemicals. All through the night, he'd pour chemicals from one vial into another, occasionally torching or freezing a mixture for good measure. Before sunrise, he'd slink away into the early morning with a new batch of secret pills and potions to try with his breakfast.

11.

"You're dead!" screamed the lumbering old blob. But Killian was too fast. He dove out of the way, easily missing the old man's tackle. The house shook when the man came crashing down.

"I'll kill you, you bastard!" yelled the old man, now throwing empty beer bottles.

Killian ducked, climbed under a table, summersaulted over a couch, jumped off a wall, grabbed hold of the light fixture, flew through the air, and landed a terrific kick right on the old man's face.

Scrambling to escape, running for his life, Killian stepped on a beer bottle. His legs whooshed into the air as he smacked down hard on his back.

Just a regular night at Killian's place.

Next somebody was sure to get spanked. Some dishes would get broken. Some tears and blood shed and spilled. There would be hours of intermittent boozing and yelling. Then finally silence. Silence so panic-stricken you'd wish for the screaming to start up again.

"You ugly shit!" yelled Killian's mom, slapping him across the face with a dish towel. "Talking about Dudebuddy at school. I ought to wring your neck!"

She put the dish towel around his neck and started wringing. Killian struggled to escape, but he was tied to a chair.

His towering pop smacked the old lady aside. Then he gripped Killian's neck with his bare hands and the wringing continued.

"Who told you about Dudebuddy! Don't you know that's the devil? Don't you know that could get us all shot like pigs?!"

The old lady was back. She took turns smacking Killian's face and pounding on the old man.

"If I ever—" smack! "hear of you—" smack! "saying that word again—" smack! ...SMACK!

12.

It was like the whole room exploded. Everything flashed white, then went black. Except it wasn't black—it was purple. Dark purple in the form of smoke.

The smoke cleared, revealing the figure of a man in a lab coat with a crazed look in his eyes. It was Uncle Jon, hands on hips.

"Leave that boy alone," said Uncle Jon.

"Bursting into my house! Smokin' up my den!" hollered the old man, coughing. "Come 'ere, I'll break your chicken face!"

Uncle Jon stood his ground. He raised a hand and did a flick. Next thing, an explosion erupted directly under the old man, sending him sailing up against the ceiling. He crashed down unconscious in a heap of smoking fat.

"Wahhh!" yelled the old lady, running madly away on all fours.

"Come on, buddy," said Uncle Jon, untying Killian. "Let's get out of here, huh?"

13.

Interview with a Caucasian landowner, pt. 1: "At the Casino" (WARNING: This interview series is unedited. Anyone likely to be offended by a privileged-ass white guy going off about politics is advised to take a nice, long, scenic drive through the Catskills.)

INTERVIEWER: How're you feeling tonight? Think you'll win big?

CAUCASION LANDOWNER: Man, winin' big is for suckers. I'm just here to kick some ass.

I: And is craps your favorite game?

CL: It's not a damn game. Jesus! And quiet a sec. I got to focus.

I: Alright, well…

CL: Come on, come on. …Yeah! Woooh! See that, champ?! You see that?!

I: Nice!

CL: Okay. Let's ditch this kid stuff and go find us something to *drank*.

I: How do you feel about the current political landscape?

CL: Damn, will you look at the ass on that!

I: Actually, I'm gay, so… But, sure, not bad.

CL: Fuck it, bud, everybody's a little homo. What I'm talking about…I'm talking about quality of a good hump. Eyes closed, lights off, tell me you wouldn't be in for a good hump sesh with that?

I: In the recent election cycle, were you surprised by any of the results?

CL: What do you mean "surprised"?

I: On a scale of one to ten, ten being utterly shocked.

CL: Zero. Nothing surprises me—ever.

I: Did you vote for Robbie Cox?

CL: Robbie Cox? Ha, ha! What the hell type a name is that? Don't know who the hell would even bother to run for politics with a name like that.

I: His name has been all over the news every day this week.

He won a very important position in the World Senate.

CL: He won?

I: Did you even vote?

CL: Of course I voted, you jackass! How can you even ask that and expect to not get socked in the face? You damn prick!

I: What's your process in terms of choosing a candidate to vote for?

CL: I'm drinking bourbon neat. Drinks on me. What you having, some kinda girlie thing?

14.

Homunculus Castle is perched the same place it's been for the past few thousand years—way high up in the mountains in Central Europe. But now it has a brand new driveway winding 70 miles through perilous ravines and along mountainous vistas. Eleanor George oversaw construction of the new driveway—finished just in time for this year's meeting of all the world's leaders.

Imagine all the superheroes getting together in one place! It's like the most amazing party ever! Gossip for days!

First it was just a rumor. No one but an idiot could actually believe that something so exciting could really happen. An annual meeting of all the most powerful superheroes? No way!

Decades went by and it was still just a rumor. The mystery made it extra exciting. But then, one year, some jerk on the waitstaff gave a tip-off to the local news stations. Right away, it was a zoo. And it's been that way ever since. News people coming from across the world just to glimpse the big names in politics.

"You can't have a proper castle without a respectable drive-way," Eleanor George said at last, at the driveway opening ceremony, to a flock of press.

King Homunculus might possibly have disagreed. But who cares? He's been dead so long, he wouldn't even know the first thing about modern publicity.

15.

INTERNATIONAL NEWS AND POLITICS REPORT: Robbie Cox was spotted driving along the mountainous vistas on the newly completed Homunculus Castle driveway. Other superheroes are expected to arrive within the coming days. News anchors are camped outside the driveway gate, thousands of them, ready for the most highly anticipated event of the year.

16.

"What's this thing?" asked Killian.

"That's a pipeclay triangle," said Uncle Jon.

"What's it do?"

"It's for holding a little crucible—that's this thing. Like this, you hold it over a Bunsen burner. See?" Uncle Jon demonstrated.

"Woah..."

Killian had never seen a real science lab before. He felt like a knight going through an ancient war room, viewing each instrument as a devastating weapon with secret powers.

"Now what do you think this is?" asked Uncle Jon, holding up a particular item.

"Another beaker?"

"Sort of! Except the ones with this shape are called Erlenmeyer flasks."

Killian held one of the flasks and studied it carefully. "Is this what you used to blow up my dad?"

Uncle Jon let out a sciency laugh. "No! Tee-hee! No, no! But I did use them when I mixed the potion! How did you know?" and he patted Killian's head with affection.

17.

Time to save the world—once again! Here's the agenda at the world leaders' conference. Day 1: Pick out the most urgent ways in which the world will certainly be annihilated at any moment. Day 2: Make plans to save the world.

It looked to be a pretty routine Day 1. The politicians were gathered in the ancient theater at the heart of Homunculus Castle. Sweet Jesus stood behind the podium. The eldest of the world leaders, he was a longtime fixture of the conference. Most of his superpowers had faded by this time, but he could still operate a projector with a good deal of competence. Most half-blind old drunks his age would be at an utter loss before a crowd of this stature.

"Sweet Jesus, I'd like to call attention to super virus Ignisverumitten. Better known as Erectalphlegm Syndrome." This came from a square-headed, thick-chested politician from California, name of Kyle Rick-Jones.

Behind the podium, Sweet Jesus added the new item to the list projected on the slide. It was item #87 of potential ways in which the world will certainly be annihilated.

"Spell it!" said Sweet Jesus.

"Erectalphlegm. E, R, E, C, T, A, L, P, H, L, E, G, M. Syndrome.

S, Y, N, D, R, O, M, E."

"Uh-huh, uh-huh. Now, attributes of certain doom?"

Kyle Rick-Jones cleared his throat. Stroking his ultra-square chin, he read down the list of applicable attributes of certain doom:

"Recently thawed-out virus from arctic glaciers, so it's primordial. Two, it's a giant virus, or Megavirales, meaning it's significantly larger and more psychologically perturbing than your garden variety virus-type. Three, there's no known medication for it and no research is being done. Four, it's molecular structure is—"

"So what happens when you catch the damn thing?" Sweet Jesus interjected. This was about the tenth giant virus brought up so far. It was turning into a regular giant virus convention.

"Okay, yes, so: There has only been one known case of an infected person. It was one of the scientists handling the virus after it was first discovered. Less than 48 hours after infection, he grew an erection of unnatural proportions that began to spew a peculiar orange-tinted phlegm, the toxicity of which was reportedly catastrophic: think more radio active than plutonium, more acidic than sulfuric acid.

"The infected scientist's corpse spewed the phlegm long after he died. It's unknown whether or not the phlegm itself is contagious. However, it's estimated that...if half a million men were to contract the virus within a ten-mile radius, enough toxic phlegm would be created to spark a nuclear reaction that could potentially blow up the entire planet."

"Uh-huh, uh-huh," said Sweet Jesus. He looked around the room. "Okay, who's next?"

18.

The legend of Homunculus Castle. Going way back. Long before voting or the corollary of groupthink. Right about when politics crawled out of the antediluvian sewage, naked, dripping slime, whimpering for a suckling at the tit.

Warfare brought about politics coming into adolescence, up from toddlerhood and battling with sticks. Resources for the first time were divvied up based on an advanced political concept: spoils.

Then came the giants. Not just any giants, but the giants that killed the lesser giants. The giant giant killers.

These extra large, extra strong world-conquerors battled throughout the four corners, each venturing off in his own direction. Until they arrived simultaneously at a particularly magical land of perilous ravines and mountainous vistas. Surveying the whole world from the tallest peak, each giant shared his story of the many territories he had conquered. Together, they celebrated their victories.

Desiring to establish a central fortress from which the world could be governed, the giants began to construct a castle in the mountains. Their peaceful relations, however, were short-lived. None of the giants wanted to actually work—instead, they were each inclined to instruct the others in carrying out the building process. After centuries of supposed construction on the central fortress, not a single stone had been laid.

Frustrated beyond words, the giants then began to wage physical assaults upon one another. Their petty feuds quickly escalated into a full-scale war. It was the Great War of the Giant Giants. Or the Giant War of the Great Giants. Or the Giant Giant War of the Greats. According to legend, each of these three possible titles of the war are correct—or at least close enough.

The war raged on and on. None of the giants ever gained the upper hand. Using the peaks of the mounts as weapons, they hacked away at each other day and night. As the decades of war went by, the giants ultimately hacked each other into smaller and smaller bits. Finally, right around the dawn of ancient history, the giants had hacked themselves down to the size of average-sized ants. They were no longer fit to call themselves giants.

One day, all the mini, hacked-up versions of the original giants gathered together to evaluate their situation. Since they were now so small and weak individually, they agreed that they'd have to join together if they were to maintain their ruling status over the world. So that's what they did.

As their first order of business, they built a castle—a castle so large and beautiful as to be suitable not only for a giant, but a giant giant killer. A castle so large and beautiful—also—as to attract the loveliest princesses from throughout the land. And that was how Homunculus Castle came to be built.

Unfortunately for the homunculi ("little men"), when a princess finally arrived, they were all too small to catch her attention, let alone impregnate her. Instead, a rather normal prince came on the scene and made normal-sized babies with her. The time of the giants was finished, but they still lived on in the spirit of their politics, their war strategies, and of course their castle.

19.

A group of bearded guys in terrycloth bathrobes gathered on a city street corner. They stood there holding up signs to the oncoming traffic. Their beards blew in the wind, but their signs held steady.

Their signs read: LIBERATE DUDEBUDDY.

Most people driving by had no idea what the signs meant. A few had vague inklings.

The bearded guys stood there all day.

In the evening, a cop stopped with hands on hips. "Alright, let's move it along."

The bearded guys slowly turned their heads. They looked blankly at the cop. Their beards were still. The wind had ceased to blow. "Liberate Dudebuddy," said one of the them.

The cop felt an odd chill run down his spine. He mumbled something under his breath and then moved on.

The next day, the street corner was vacant, as if there had never been a rally of bearded guys holding protest signs, as if everyone in the city had just imaged it.

20.

Every kid's favorite cartoon show came on at 10 a.m. It was the most popular show anywhere: yesterday's news, animated.

A burning building! The fire leapt across the street to the roof of a gas station! The flames—glowing yellow and neon red!—crept over the edge of the roof and climbed down toward the pumps... People ran off screaming! One guy couldn't start his car! He turned the key again and again...nothing! The flames were coming! They licked at his wheels... Teased toward the pumps...!

Can no one help this poor guy? If the fire gets to the pumps, will it be too late for him? For the whole neighborhood? How many lives will be lost? Tens...? Hundreds...?

Just then, Francine Dixon, city council member from the third district, raced onto the scene. Within moments, she had the situation scoped out—she had a plan. Dipping her long, blonde hair into the nearest container of window washer fluid, she went straight into the flames. Swinging her head around and around like a sideways helicopter, she slashed into the fire with her soaking hair. Soon, the flames were beaten back from the pumps. The crowd that had gathered began to cheer.

Finally the fire trucks arrived. Francine joined the fire fighters as they dowsed the last of the flames.

"Francine Dixon, council member, saves the day!" said a cartoon version of the real-life news reporter.

21.

"We interrupt this episode of political cartoon news hour to bring you an official update LIVE from Homunculus Castle."

Kids everywhere lurched backwards, thrown off to have cartoon hour interrupted by a real person.

Real news anchor Ted Mac stood broadcasting before the castle moat.

"The world leaders have reached a final agreement," said Mac. "They have selected a total of ten ways in which life on Earth could be annihilated at any moment. The actual list hasn't been released yet, but our sources indicated that we can expect to hear about at least several giant viruses. There's also rumored to be an asteroid, at least one terrorist group, and yet another threat of annihilation from machines taking over! No news yet whether an alien invasion   made this year's list..."

A swirl of bright colors brought everybody back to cartoon land.

"Cool!" said an excited purple octopus. "Sounds like the politicians got a lot to do!" The octopus wiggled its tentacles and did a little dance.

"Ah, so what," said a grouchy hippopotamus. "It's only the whole world at stake. No biggie, jeez."

"Oh yeah?" countered the octopus. "Then why dontcha just go join up with the giant viruses, or the terrorists, or the evil machines, huh? Huh?!"

"Well, you know what?" muttered the hippo. "Maybe I just will..."

Then the hippo became dismembered, and each of its various parts became different things, either viruses, terrorists, or evil machines. This all happened in about a second and a half.

"Eeeeeek!" screamed the octopus, its legs spinning and flailing. The viruses, terrorists, and machines were almost too fast, but just in time the octopus zipped away in a spray of black ink.

22.

Killian turned off the TV at Uncle Jon's place. Everything was boring. Uncle Jon was at work. There was nothing to do. This place was dull. Wasn't there at least something to eat?

For the first time ever, Killian almost wished he were at school. It was the middle of the day. What's there to do during the middle of the day? Might as well be doing something you don't like so at least you can dream of being somewhere else. School's perfect for that. Being at your uncle's house? That's just neutral. You're stuck dreaming of being miserable so you can dream of being free.

Suddenly Killian had a thought. Was he kidnapped?

23.

The two monarchs, Al and Charlie, were drunk. They'd been drinking all day and all night for weeks. By this time, they were no longer on their barstools. Now they were upstairs in the whores' chambers: two conjoined bedrooms, a closet, a wash room.

In one room, Charlie lay in bed hogging all the blankets. He dreamed about the next time he'd get up and go use the toilet. In his dream, he was getting pretty close to needing to go. It wouldn't be much longer now...

In the other room, Tracy and Meg had tied Al up to the bedpost. Tracy wore Charlie's crown. Once Al was securely fastened to the bedpost, Meg reached for Al's crown. She plucked it off his head with money signs dancing in her eyes.

Al was so drunk he didn't put up a fight. In his drunken state, all he could focus on was trying not to puke. The girls kept leaning over in his face as they tied him up. He couldn't help picturing his full guts' worth of toxic, boozy puke splashing right between their breasts.

Right as Meg took the crown, Al heaved. He tried to gulp it down but couldn't. Up it came, hot and horrible, covering Meg's hands, splashing on her face, running all the way down her white corset.

It sounded like two banshees screeching from a distant cavern. In the next room, in Charlie's dream, that was the image: a two-headed banshee screeching from the entrance of some hellish cave. The banshee had bat wings and a dragon tail.

Charlie flopped his arms and yelped back like a defenseless, frightened crow. In the form of a crow fleeing the banshees, fat and sort of scrambling through the air to get away, his bladder began to empty. He flew faster with the lighter load.

"My corset! It's ruined!" screamed Tracy between banshee cries.

"I'm soaked! It's all down my tits!" Meg shrieked, shaking her hands and jumping up and down.

They began to strip, undoing their corsets as frantically as possibly in a convulsive striptease.

As their corsets were just coming off, and as Al began a second round of heaves, a river of warm yellow liquid began to flow around the girls' ankles. A moment later it was up to their calves, then their knees. They were so preoccupied with dodging the new shots of puke that they didn't notice the river of piss until it was up to their thighs. Suddenly they were naked, swimming in piss.

Charlie appeared in the doorway. He was groggy-eyed but otherwise seemed unconcerned about having to wade through the yellow waters.

"Looks like somebody's been having fun," said Charlie, admiring the knots around Al's feet, wrists, and neck. He looked around for the girls, but apparently they had been washed away.

After untying Al, Charlie fished out the crowns from the dissipating river. He placed the crowns back where they belonged—on the sovereign heads of monarchs. Both crowns glistened like newly-washing gold with a just hint of sparkling piss yellow.

24.

Eleanor George was very often illusive and mysterious in her actions. She was so high up in the politics business, yet so far removed from practical concerns, that it was difficult to gauge exactly what role she played—especially on a day-to-day basis.

But recently, it seemed as though she had all but withdrawn from her dealings in politics. This hadn't caught the attention of many, but it wasn't missed by Sweet Jesus, who called late one night to pressure her into taking a stance on the new list of urgent crises facing the world.

"I'm not convinced, Sweet Jesus," said Eleanor. She shook her head. Although it was late, she was still in her office at Global Media Headquarters, way up high in her skyscraper with London's financial district twinkling on all sides far below.

Sweet Jesus was on the phone. He was being defensive as hell, which wasn't exactly a surprise. He was at that age when he could finally be honest. Yelling at his superiors was now his favorite thing. So what if he'd get fired? Sure, fire him! Let him die in peace!

Defending himself, Sweet Jesus yelled, "Wait till the giant viruses make their move! They're coming, my dear. Sure as hell!"

Eleanor turned down her phone's volume. "When are they coming?"

"Any day now! Far as I know, their first stop is with London's financial haut monde! If I were you, I'd have some precautions in place already! You wearing gloves and a mask? Breathing filtered air? Perhaps you ought to be!"

Eleanor relaxed into her desk chair. At her fingertips: the list of this year's top ten ways in which the world would certainly end at any moment. Glancing through the details, she smiled ever so slightly.

No one had seen the list yet. Only the world leaders and Sweet Jesus. Now they were awaiting orders from Eleanor. She owned that much of the media. What people see on the news would have to make good cartoon shows the next day. The cartoon shows would have to make good comic books, which would have to make good movies, which would have to propel the sales of toys, clothes, accessories, and amusement park rides.

While the average consumer was thinking about how the world would end, Eleanor had to consider the possible ticket sales of movie sequels. At least Sweet Jesus got that.

"Okay," said Eleanor. "If the super viruses are going to come at any moment, then let them. Until then, there's no use taking action. These threats aren't worth the trouble."

25.

Killian couldn't sleep. All morning he'd watched updates on the ten threats to the world. Then nothing. The updates stopped. It was like everybody just forgot all about making plans to save the world. First the cartoons made it sound like the world was going to end at any second, and then...what? Suddenly nothing to worry about?

It didn't seem right. Killian wanted to ask Uncle Jon about it, but he couldn't. Uncle Jon had been acting strange recently. He never spoke anymore. Just mumbled about politics sometimes. Nothing that ever made sense.

Adults never made sense when they talked about politics. Politics is a thing for kids! Only kids understand superpowers and the evilness of evil. Kids, if they had the choice, would never let the world end! They'd save it every time!

But kids can't save the world. They have to wait. They can't even vote. All they can do is wait and hope that the world doesn't end before they get a chance to vote and change things themselves.

Good luck getting to sleep at this rate, Killian thought to himself. He was all worked up. And convinced the world was going to end at any moment.

Ten... Nine... Eight...

It was like that for hours. An endless countdown.

Then Killian heard a noise. It sounded like the front door closing. He got up to peek out the window. It was Uncle Jon leaving. But where was he going this early?

Killian got dressed as quickly as possible. He threw on pants, whispering to himself, "No way, no he doesn't... He can't just up and leave me here all alone as the world ends."

26.

Three... Two... One... Nothing! But still, any second now!

Killian ran all the way to Uncle Jon's work at the big science lab. Sure enough, Uncle Jon's truck was parked in the lot.

No use trying to get inside, thought Killian...but that doesn't mean I can't peek inside.

The building was a typical cement structure in an aging business park: two stories, cold cement façade, long windows at regular intervals. The landscaping was as soulless as the building: a few trees, a few shrubberies, gravel.

Just like in the cartoons, Killian thought as he crept around in the dark, looking for signs of life, or lights, or security cameras. After his long run, his heart was pumping in his ears like a triumphant workout beat. He had the adrenaline of rocket fuel.

Dudebuddy knows, he thought. Dudebuddy knows when the world will end.

None of the windows had lights on. But he peeked in all of them. When there was nothing to see on the ground floor, he climbed up the side of the building to the peek in the top floor windows.

At the far corner of the building, hanging on with aching fingers and arms about to give out, Killian glimpsed something moving. It was definitely a person. He ducked down and stared intently. Inside was an expansive lab room. Nothing out of the ordinary except a head-shaped thing hovering over a microscope. It was Uncle Jon all right. But what was he doing in there with all the lights off?

27.

Interview with a Caucasian landowner, pt. 2: "At the Football Game" (WARNING: This interview series is unedited. Anyone possibly offended by a pale-skinned hick going off about politics is advised to take a healthy dose of Xanax.)

INTERVIEWER: This is your favorite sport, huh—football?

CAUCASION LANDOWNER: Favorites are for pussies. Unless you're talking about what's actually better than everything else. In that case, yeah, football's my favorite. It's just the best game there is.

I: What do you imagine is the biggest threat to the world at this moment?

CL: Taxes!

I: So, taxes are going to destroy the world at any moment?

CL: Well, guess I never thought of it like that, man. But, now that you said it first, sounds not too far off from the truth.

I: And you would save the world by...?

CL: Tax anything...fuckin' tax the moon, for all I care. Just don't tax me!

I: What if it is, in fact, very possible the world could end at any moment?

CL: I work goddamn hard for my money! But then the government comes in and says, ah, hey, thanks sucker, we'll just go ahead and take this mega slice of pie here and how about that shirt off your back while we're at it... Pricks!

I: But all the money in the world couldn't—

CL: Wooh! Run, baby! Ah! Hey! Suck it! Kiss my landowner's ass! You see that?! See him make the thirty yard? Now we've got 'em. Kiss my ass! Kiss my ass! Game's over now, champ.

28.

In his prime, Sweet Jesus could save the world, capture the supervillains, and give the best damn television interview you've ever seen in your life—all without breaking a sweat or losing his cool.

Today he could barely keep his false teeth in straight.

If he had a political slogan for his current state of being, it would be, "Half dead can still get out of bed!"

Look at the old guy not giving up! Who wouldn't vote for that?! Whiskey in hand, breath heaving, voice hoarse as a bulldozer on volcanic rock... He was breaking a sweat and losing his cool all over the place—but his false teeth were straight, just about!

If he had a superhero tagline on a t-shirt, it would be, "What doesn't kill you makes you wait longer for the moment of truth!"

New York City. Exclusive nightclub. Very exclusive. A table in the back—so far back it's hidden behind a secret wall.

Kyle Rick-Jones, the Erectalphlegm Syndrome guy, was sitting there drinking gin. There were three others, also bigwig politicians from various countries. Each of them had introduced one of the new top ten threats to the world.

Sweet Jesus shared with his colleagues the pronouncement by Eleanor George. Do nothing, threats not worth the trouble. Let the super viruses come. So what if the world ends, she says.

Kyle Rick-Jones jumped to his feet. "We can't let that happen," he cried.

An uncomfortable silence fell over the politicians. They glanced uncertainly at each other. One of them sipped his drink and choked on it softly. They were all thinking the same thing. After a moment, Kyle Rick-Jones sat back down. He mumbled something about erectalphlegm. A big-time politician named Stuart Crane reached over and patted Kyle on the shoulder.

"You know she's right," said a voice. It was Robbie Cox, waltzing over, appearing out of the shadows.

"Who invited this jackass?" Kyle Rick-Jones muttered under his breath.

"Don't mean to interrupt," said Robbie. "This just happens to be my favorite night spot. And my favorite table."

"Please," said Sweet Jesus, "join us."

"Nah. But thanks, Sweets. Just so happens I'm not particularly into conspiring behind my employer's back. Going out on a limb here? I'd say you guys need to pull your heads out. Realize there's a bigger picture—not just your neat and tidy 'save the world' agendas. Like contracts. Who here signed a contract before taking office? That's what I thought. Why sign those contracts unless there's a greater purpose? How about marketing revenue, huh? How about television shows for kids that matter? Year over year, viewership of save-the-world events is down. If there's a theme song to modern superheroes, it's the sound of revenues swirling down a toilet bowl. Kyle Rick-Jones...you really think the world is going to end by Erectalphlegm Syndrome? Yeah, didn't think so."

29.

INTERNATIONAL NEWS AND POLITICS REPORT: Twenty-nine cases of Erectalphlegm Syndrome in Indonesia have caused a panic throughout Southeast Asia.

INTERNATIONAL NEWS AND POLITICS REPORT: Small towns in America are continuing to report casualties from a mysterious virus; no comment from the authorities.

INTERNATIONAL NEWS AND POLITICS REPORT: NASA has warned of the possibility that an asteroid is heading dangerously close to our orbit. The chances of an impact are increasing each day.

30.

Killian's sickness hit him all at once. The first of the symptoms came on the night he spied on Uncle Jon. That's how he got sick, he figured. It was from staying out too late in the cold.

The next day he lay in bed sweating, unable to sleep or eat. He felt nauseous and had every kind of ache in his bones. It was the sickest he'd ever felt. He felt so sick he figured there must be some kind of award for enduring such terrible discomfort. At any moment, he expected a team of doctors to rush in and say, "Congratulations! You're the sickest kid we've ever seen!"

But that was only the beginning. It grew worse and worse. This wasn't just any old garden-variety sickness. This sickness had its own special key card to the pain centers. A sore erupting on the back of the neck would cause the left big toe to arch back in throbbing agony. An ache in the knee caps would make the nose bleed.

Uncle Jon appeared at intervals.

"Doctor…" Killian whimpered, pleading, "I need…doctor…"

"Mm-hm," muttered Uncle Jon, taking notes. "Mm-hm."

Killian flopped off the couch, his body erupting in pain, his heartbeats growing dim, his breath shallow. He lashed out with arms and legs lunging, like trying to swim through mud. His neck contorted. Somehow never making much progress, but screaming to crawl toward Uncle Jon's ankles to beg.

"Interesting," said Uncle Jon, taking steps back. "Fascinating."

31.

Writhing at Uncle Jon's toes, Killian momentarily lurched out of his own skin. He was bodiless and frozen as Uncle Jon jabbered on about science.

There's my body, huh, thought bodiless Killian. Wow, holy cow if that's not a sick-looking kid for sure... And there's Uncle Jon, mouth moving like he's eating hot soup.

Everything was quiet, a little hazy, moving in slow motion. This must be death, thought bodiless Killian.

"You're not reflecting on the lives of the saints, are you?" asked a voice.

Something moved into focus across the room. It was a strange-looking man in a terrycloth bathrobe. He had hair down to his shoulders, a few days' scruff on his face, and an unusually care-free way of slouching, as though he were extremely comfortable all of the time.

"Best to just sit back...you know, have a beer."

Suddenly Killian noticed a beer in his bodiless hand. Not sure what to do with it, he took a sip. It was about what he'd expected. He'd never had a beer before. It was okay.

"The next thing you'll want is a proper orgy," said the strange man. "Come on," he said, motioning with a cool head nod.

Bodiless Killian started to follow the strange man, but then he looked back and noticed that his body was no longer writhing on the floor. Uncle Jon had picked up the body and was carrying it away. Not sure what to do, Killian looked in one direction and then the other. Finally he dropped the beer and went racing after his body.

32.

A desert scene at night. It would take a million spy cameras and still you'd have a difficult time seeing anything wrong with this picture. The wind picked up, tossing around the sand like play money. The cold stars intensified as the nocturnal creatures began to stir. Still you couldn't possibly see a thing wrong.

But then cloaked heads began to slowly rise out from the dunes. First one, then a whole gang of them. The cloaked heads were turned to the sky, watching an airplane flying overheard. A figure plummeted from the plane. The cloaked heads followed the figure as it fell, as a parachute opened…

The parachuter landed right among the most uncharted dunes in the desert. As the parachute fluttered to a standstill, the cloaked heads rose out of those dunes. Suddenly the parachuter was surrounded on all sides by towering men in black cloaks. The men carried swords and machine guns. Greetings were exchange in silence. Then the cloaked men led the parachuter to the nearest trap door and down they went into the heart of the world's most unknown desert caves.

"Wow, hey this is so cool!" said the parachuter upon entering the caves. In response, he was wacked in the head by a machine gun. Knocked unconscious, he was dragged by his feet the rest of the way down into the innermost chamber.

33.

Next day on the news, cartoons everywhere showed Kyle Rick-Jones strapped to a chair, gagged, dried blood caked on his face, surrounded on either side by armed guards.

The caption read: "Top Politician Captured by Terrorists!"

"Warning," said an automated voice. "The following cartoon footage is graphic and disturbing and may not be suitable for our younger viewers."

What's going on here?!

Flash to a cartoon news reporter: "An anonymous terrorist organization has apparently captured politician Kyle Rick-Jones. In a statement issued by the terrorists, Mr. Rick-Jones went to the terrorists in order to sell top-secret information about Erectalphlegm Syndrome, one of the deadliest viruses currently threatening life as we know it."

No way! A politician betraying his country...going to terrorists...peddling a virus that could almost certainly bring about the end of the world? How atrocious! Too shocking to believe! Is it possible?!

The clip from the terrorists was grainy and the lighting was terrible—even in cartoon form. Kyle Rick-Jones moaned and cried out through swollen, bloody lips. The sound was muted, so his cries were inaudible.

A spout of orange liquid suddenly sprayed up into his face. Sputtering and coughing, Kyle Rick-Jones couldn't go on. The orange spray was eating away at his flesh. His skin sizzled and melted off the bone. It was the most gruesome sight imaginable... even the guards with machine guns stepped back in horror.

34.

"I can't watch this," said Sweet Jesus.

Eating chicken broth alone at Homunculus Castle, he turned the television off and sat in dismal silence. Except for the sound he made sipping broth, which echoed throughout the stone chambers like some kind of major indoors weather occurrence. Then again, Sweet Jesus was nearly deaf.

"Kyle Rick-Jones..." he muttered at last, "good thinking, there, kid."

He got up from his seat, laughing sadly. His laughter

echoed back like someone falling down a well and drowning at the bottom.

These were the days when he washed his own dishes. Housekeepers were for kings. Sweet Jesus, nowadays, was just the caretaker of an old castle with as many rats as it had leaks.

After washing his broth bowl, he was about to head for his reading chambers when he decided to take a detour. Hobbling through a maze of hallways and ballrooms toward the front entrance, he finally made his way into the back storage area of the castle gift shop.

Way back in a dusty storage closet, he pulled out a box of old merchandise that hadn't been touched in a long time. He began to remove the ancient items one by one: Sweet Jesus action figures, Sweet Jesus postcards, Sweet Jesus shot glasses, Sweet Jesus t-shirts... There were all kinds of things. It would be impossible to say what still had value and what didn't.

Among a box full of ancient-looking documents, there was even the complete text of the Sovereign Summons—the mythical incantation for bringing about relative world peace, whatever that meant. "I think this one's a keeper," said Sweet Jesus, pocketing the ancient text as he kept on digging.

Finally he pulled out the most important item of all: a life-size Sweet Jesus superhero costume.

35.

Killian sat up from bed after a long sleep. The first thing he noticed was an uncanny lack of aches, like his whole body had been set loose from a thicket of brambles. Also his vision was clear again and he could feel his appetite returning.

Only his mind still seemed affected by some malady. He had

all these questions. Where was he? Was there a quiz today in Ms. Buckingham's class? Shouldn't he be at school already?

He couldn't remember much. Just something about a guy in a terrycloth bathrobe inviting him to—

Uncle Jon walked in.

"Ah! Hum! Isn't somebody looking better today!"

"Yeah."

"So how is the little invalid?"

"Okay."

"Hungry?"

"Sure."

"I'll grab you some donuts and fruit. But first..." Uncle Jon approach with a big needle. "Just a little shot."

"What's that for?"

"It's to make you well. Very last dose today. Good boy!"

36.

Robbie Cox was air boxing like a real champ when Eleanor George entered the room wearing the skimpiest lingerie in politics. Dainty piano music played in the background and candlelight flickered upon exquisite paintings of various high points in political history. Only the best of the best ever made its way into this highly exclusive and practically sacred chamber, which was Eleanor George's bedroom.

Robbie Cox did one more right-hook in the air and then accepted the champagne flute.

"Thanks, babe," he said.

"To the grand finale, darling."

"You've been saying that a lot lately," he observed before gulping down the whole flute. He went to help himself to the bottle.

"Come here," Eleanor instructed. She caught up with Robbie in the center of the room. He was holding the bottle and she was playing with the little lacy bow on her chest. "You'll know what I mean in a minute."

"I just figured you were talking about Kyle Rick-Jones."

"I was last time I toasted to a grand finale."

"Over beers at the club."

"The opera. And you had a beer, yes."

"What's wrong with beer? It's an ancient, historical beverage, going back to the Egyptians. Pretty sure there were at least a few gods who took sacrifices with their beer."

"Gods never knew the first thing about campaigns, lobbying, bribery..."

"If I were a god, I'd be a beer god for sure."

They started kissing. Robbie picked Eleanor up off the ground, held her in his arms, then lifted her above his head and did a few quick reps before tossing her down onto the bed.

37.

So get this! The ancient documents about Dudebuddy Nation? One of them has been found!

Oh, hi. It's the copyeditors, by the way.

So, one of the stolen boxes turned up. It's unclear at this point exactly how excited we should be about this "find." But we're going to go ahead and be pretty freaking jazzed. Let's face it, this job ain't the world's most riveting. Let us enjoy a moment of excitement, okay? Even if it is most likely a false alarm.

What we know so far: one box found, containing at least a slim but non-empty folder. We're guessing the papers in that folder aren't just pictures of cats licking themselves. If there's writing on the papers, we can only hope that it's in a language someone around here can translate.

Beyond that, we're in the dark, per usual.

38.

Killian watched Uncle Jon drive away. Standing on the doorstep of his home, he felt homeless. Knocking to have the door answered by his parents, he felt like he didn't have a family.

In fact, no one answered, so he let himself in through an open window. It was dead silent inside but there were lights on. He thought about calling out to see if anyone was there, but instead decided to keep quiet.

On tiptoes, he walked down the hall and into the kitchen. His mom was there, passed out drunk on the floor and snoring like a fatigued cow. Killian tiptoed on by.

In the living room, he found his pop, or what was left of him. Lying on the couch, the old guy was wrapped in all sorts of slings, make-shift casts, and bandages. His entire face was covered in an off-white, blood-stained medical wrap. As Killian made his way through the living room and on to his bedroom, he felt the grim, freakishly alive eyes of his father following him, judging.

The air was different in his bedroom. It was stale as if everything had lost its color under a layer of gray dust. Except there was no dust, really. Not any more than usual, anyway. And the walls were still covered with the vibrant posters of superheroes.

Something had to change. Impulsively, but still as quietly as possible, Killian tore down all the posters. That was better.

39.

Interview with a Caucasian landowner, pt. 3: "Boating" (WARNING: This interview series is unedited. Anyone possibly offended by a pastyfaced white guy harping on about politics is advised to reconnect with the pleasures of childhood comfort food.)

INTERVIEWER: It's so beautiful out here on the lake. Absolutely stunning!

CAUCASION LANDOWNER: Bet you won't be saying that after catching third degree sun burns, bud.

I: On a scale of one to ten, how demoralized do you feel about the death of Kyle Rick-Jones?

CL: Always knew he was a terrorist. Easy. Next question!

I: But on the scale...

CL: What scale?

I: One to ten, how demoralized do you feel?

CL: Ten doesn't even come close. It's off the damn charts! Not that I was surprised at all. Practically saw that one coming.

I: You mean even his cause of death? Certainly that was a bit of a shock!

CL: Truth is, swear to Saint Joe, all that orange jizz on his face is pretty much exactly how I pictured him...ya know... signing off.

I: In your opinion, is the establishment letting down the common voter?

CL: You're going to have to go ask the "common voter" yourself if you want an answer to that, ha, ha. How's that sun burn setting in?

I: Isn't this taking it a bit fast around the turn?

CL: What's that, bro?

I: AHHHH!!!!!!

CL: WOOOH!!!!!

I: Can you just drop me off at the shore?

CL: Wasn't that a fuckin' rush?

I: Right over there is fine.

CL: You don't want to go over there.

I: Why not?

CL: Starboard.

I: What?

CL: Starboard. There. Chicks on the boat, man.

I: What are you doing?

CL: Just going to glide by.

I: You're going too fast.

CL: Nah. Just play cool. I got this.

I: Oh God…

CL: Ha! Ha! Ha!

I: That was too close.

CL: Hey, ladies! Which one of you wants to help me take this thing up to full speed?

BIKINI GIRL: I'll take a ride!

CL: Ha, ha! Hop in! Plenty of room.

BG: So how fast does this thing go?

CL: Fast enough.

BG: How fast?

CL: You just wait. First we take her nice and easy.

BG: Actually, you better take me back. My boyfriend…

CL: Your what?

BG: My boyfriend. I think he's…

CL: What's that? Can't hear ya! Just getting her up to speed here!

I: Do you ever have a sneaking suspicion that politicians are a bad influence on the general public?

CL: Don't mind this guy, babe, he's just here to…well, whatever. Hey, you're not into politics or anything, are you?

BG: No, not really.

CL: Good! Me neither. Cheers to that.

BG: Only when they have a really big rescue. Like when the world is going to end. Otherwise I don't pay much attention.

CL: What's that? Come up here closer so I can hear ya!

I: Is this full speed yet?

CL: Don't worry, champ! You'll know it when you see it!

40.

INTERNATIONAL NEWS AND POLITICS REPORT: Militant King X is confirmed as the killer of Kyle Rick-Jones. Anti-terrorist leaders believe the radical demigod is plotting to infect the civilized world's populace with Erectalphlegm Syndrome at any moment.

41.

POLITICAL OP-ED: Politicians are superheroes! I've seen this plastered on billboards, sung on the radio, explained in cartoons, and discussed on the subway ad nauseum—all within the past half hour. It's the one universal truth. It's the most comforting thought before bed and the only thought you need to help you get up in the morning without fear of any kind if you're like me—the nervous type. Sure, bad things happen, but when they do, the politicians will always be there to make things right. That's what they do; that's who they are: superheroes.

When I see these extra-bleak news reports (and haven't

there been a lot of them lately?), I can't help but to suspect there might be a real conspiracy happening in the media. If we were really facing some serious danger, the politicians would be all over it before you could say Sweet Jesus. Instead, we have more and more terrible news stories, and fewer and fewer incidences of politicians taking action. While the obvious reaction might be to fly off the handle about politicians failing in their duties, the more reasonable reaction (in this op-ed writer's opinion) is to question the media.

While the tragedy of Kyle Rick-Jones might have some validity, the rest of the recent stories in the news seem to be based on pure speculation. Until I see real numbers of death tolls rising from disease, until I actually see alien ships landing or burning hot fireballs shooting toward the Earth, I'm standing by the superheroes.

42.

NOTES FROM A GET WELL SOON CARD

TOM: Get will soon and then come back and give me the bug so I can stay home and skip all the stupid quizzes.

JENNY: If you're really sick, I hope you get to meet lots of politicians. But I haven't seen you in the cartoons getting saved, so I bet you're just faking. Lucky!

IAN: Jenny's been writing you love notes and Wardie's been stealing them and when I tried to stop him he punched me so now you owe me!

WARDIE: Good luck with the erektal flem ha ha.

43.

"I want everyone to welcome Killian back to class," said Ms. Buckingham.

"Welcome back, Killian," said the class in chorus.

"When I found out you were sick," said the teacher, "we made you a get well soon card."

Killian accepted the card with a shy smile. Ms. Buckingham bent down close and said, "When I sent this card to your home, it came back unopened. I was told that maybe you weren't staying at home while you were sick?"

Killian nodded vaguely.

"There's nothing the matter with your home life, is there?"

Killian lowered his eyes, shook his head. "No..."

"Okay, well you can always tell me." Then she stood up and said cheerfully. "Now, class, let's get our pencils ready for today's quiz!"

While opening the card, Killian thought about his home life... He couldn't think about it for very long before getting upset, so his mind turned to Uncle Jon. The card reminded him: he hadn't gotten sick until he went to Uncle Jon's... And he had almost died, except that Uncle Jon had a special cure...

When Killian finished reading the card, he noticed Jenny looking back at him with a smile. Then he noticed Wardie inching his desk closer to Jenny's. But there was no time to think about that. Ms. Buckingham had just handed him a quiz on algebra.

1. What's the value of $5a + 2b$ when $a = 6$ and $b = 2$?

Killian tapped his pencil on the desk. "Dudebuddy," he thought.

44.

From its perch in the treetops one early morning, a monkey looked down at the jungle floor and spied a shiny thing. Swinging down from one branch to another, it landed on the jungle floor right at the feet of two sleeping monarchs, Charlie and Al.

Al had his crown held between his arms like a soft and cuddly stuffed honey bear. But Charlie's crown lay right out in the open. The crown caught a ray of sunlight in one of its rubies. That's what had caught the monkey's attention. That incredible sparkle.

The monkey's eyes grew bigger and bigger. Slowly, the monkey reached out its paw.

Just then a second monkey swung down from the trees and tackled the first monkey. Both monkeys yelped and howled, clawed and bit each other as they fought for Charlie's crown.

"Ah...AHH!" cried Charlie, waking up with two frisky monkeys wrestling on his face.

"What? Oh God!" cried Al, jumping to his feet.

"My crown!" Charlie yelled, joining in the wrestling match.

Not willing to jeopardize the safety of his own crown, Al stood back and watched the fight. He cheered on his royal companion with his most sporting hoots and battle cries, also offering a kick at a monkey's ribs when convenient.

At last it seemed the monkeys had had enough. First one of the monkeys darted away and then the second followed close on its tail. Charlie and Al both yelled curses and taunts as the monkeys fled. Triumphant, Charlie held his crown up in the air and let out an especially loud victory shout.

But then his mood changed. He held his crown gingerly with both hands to inspect it. Something seemed wrong. Its sparkle was off.

"What's the matter, Charlie? Not scratched, I hope?"

"Monkeys took a ruby. The last one."

"Well, appears you still have diamonds to spare. Could have been much worse."

"My last ruby..." Charlie moaned.

"Stupid monkeys," said Al.

"The only thing I hate worse than monkeys," said Charlie, "is peasants."

45.

Eleanor George sat watching the news for hours. Not regular news, but local news from stations out of places like African villages, Peruvian villages, Indian villages, and Mongolian villages. Little tiny stations that no one in the superhero news racket would ever bother to purchase. Incrementally downing one of her prized wines, Eleanor soaked it all in—all the most dire news stories that no one ever heard about.

"More than half the population of the Yolajiji tribe has been wiped out by a mysterious plague... The surviving members are struggling through the worst famine on record as the plague has decimated the livestock throughout the region..."

That's how the stories went.

Sometimes a prophet or local sage would appear in a village meeting area with arms flapping to make a pronouncement.

"The gods have spoken! The end has come! He who is pure among us come sacrifice yourself and everyone you know before it's too late!"

Of course nobody these days wants to admit purity, not even in the world's remote villages. So there weren't many sacrifices. But at least a few of the most ancient sages out there were diplomatic enough to volunteer themselves to their gods' bloodlust. Eleanor watched it all. The ancient sages' selfbeheadings and everything.

"A savior is coming!" said a few of the news channels, interviewing crystal ball readers or other mystics. "We must look to the heavens for an answer!"

"Yes, quite so," laughed Eleanor, sloshing back some wine as if in celebration.

46.

Killian sat up in bed in a panic. Across the room, glowing ever so slightly, sat the strange-looking man in a terrycloth bathrobe.

"Don't mind me," said the man. "Go back to sleep, kid."

That's when Killian remembered what he had panicked about in the first place: the terrycloth bathrobe guy in his dream.

"So it wasn't a dream?" Killian asked.

"Yeah, it was a dream," said the man. "That's why you should go back to it. In dreams, I can say more without having to bother speaking in complete sentences."

"Who are you?"

"You really want to know?"

"Yes."

"Alright. Go back to sleep then and I'll tell you," said the man, his presence now towering over Killian. It was like the man took up the entire room.

"How do you want it explained?" asked the man. "With allegorical images? With a black-and-white drama? With an epic battle scene? Any particular background music you like to hear while getting all your most profound questions answered? How about something in dreamland to snack on while you enjoy the show? Some donuts with fresh fruit and chocolate milk, maybe?"

"Some..." Killian mumbled, drifting off to sleep, "donuts..."

47.

Sweet Jesus made it to London at sundown. He wanted to believe that he was right on time. In his old age—too old to receive official orders or even to fall in love if he tried—he needed this: something to do. And not just anything, but something exciting. Something no one would expect. Something he couldn't even put his finger on himself.

If it all added up to nothing more than following in the footsteps of Kyle Rick-Jones, then that's how it would be. The way things were going, the world was going to end anyway.

Off the plane, Sweet Jesus took the long ride on the Tube to the financial district. He didn't have any luggage, just the clothes on his back, his passport, and a small briefcase containing his superhero outfit.

While riding the Tube, he had a real sense of being that guy who goes undercover to save the world. Except the ride seemed to take forever, so it was like going to save the world in ultra slow motion.

At long last he found himself in the heart of the financial district. Checking the time, it was quite a bit later than he might have wanted under ideal circumstances. But then again, that was all the more reason to feel good about this exploit. The superhero, after all, always shows up right in the nick of time—for God's sake, never early!

He had a few pints in a pub to calm his nerves. A rebroadcast of highlights from an inconsequential rugby match brought everything back into perspective. Politics is just one little sector of life; it's not everything. These rugby guys—what do they care about politics? Not much. One might say that they're even superheroes in their own right.

Actually, no. That's going a bit far.

Sweet Jesus ended up good and drunk.

"Ah, fuck it all anyway," he thought to himself. "World's going to end sometime anyway, right old boy? Cheers…" And he downed another one.

The hour ticked by and the sports segment ended. As the pub crowd began to thin, a serious-minded fellow on his first drink for the night changed the channel to one of the major politics channels.

Hunkered over the bar with a fresh stout in hand, Sweet Jesus almost felt his back go out as clips from Kyle Rick-Jones's funeral were shown. Then the political correspondents transitioned to giving updates about the Erectalphlegm situation. It seemed that Militant King X was making good on his promises to spring the giant virus in the world's major cities. Oh well. The world is never going to actually end, of course, so let's just get on with the programming, shall we?

That seemed to be the tone of the broadcast.

The mood of the pub didn't quite correspond. It grew somber fast, as if everyone suspected that Erectalphlegm Syndrome was waltzing down the street a few blocks away, and any moment it might poke its sleazy orange head in for a drink, take a seat next to you at the bar, and slip its slithery tentacles down the front of your pants.

Sweet Jesus rose out of his chair. Time to go. Stumbling toward the exit, everyone eyed him suspiciously and cleared the way.

"Is that Sweet Jesus?" someone murmured. "He's not looking so good."

48.

Lingerie draped and flowing, a stream of white silk, any moment ready to fly open. Candlelight flickering off tall glass walls. Like the room was one colossal champagne bottle.

She had her breasts pretty well exposed for the screen and for that matter for anyone who might have been watching from outside, one-hundred floors up in the sky.

"The death count is already terrifying," she said like a childish flirt, leaning closer to the screen.

"But ze deadz are in small villages only," came the reply, sounding distinctly Arabic. "And ze numbers have not yet reached ze news."

"No, not yet."

"Why izzat?"

"It's too soon. First we need to see how it spreads, how quickly it kills."

"I hab seen blenty."

"Wait till you see the numbers. ...Or," Eleanor purred, pausing dramatically, "would you like to see something else?"

The satin on her shoulders slipped. She looked down, tilting her chin to the side, then looked up at the screen. Really looked into it, still wanting to get more of a reaction.

And she did, but not from the screen.

"I'll call you right back," said Eleanor George. She adjusted her gown and tapped the screen, turning it off.

Staring at her out the window a hundred stories up. Not just staring, but wobbling out of balance and just about to fall.

Gripping on the ledge by a few toes and maybe two fingers.

The problem was, his mask had flown off in the high winds. It was a cheap imitation mask. The real thing would never have done that. He would have been virtually invisible in the night. Able to scale buildings and jump from one to the next and occasionally do acrobatics midair—sight unseen, mask glued on tight, the one and only.

"Sweet Jesus," said Eleanor.

He couldn't hear her through the glass, but he could read her lips.

"Well, hello, you old hag," he answered.

She couldn't hear him through the glass, either, but she wasn't listening, anyway.

"Your goose is cooked," she said.

He wasn't sure whether to climb down or to climb up. All he knew was he wanted to get out of this situation fast. For old times' sake, he climbed up.

49.

INTERNATIONAL NEWS AND POLITICS REPORT: Eleanor George terminated the contract of Sweet Jesus. Now Sweet Jesus must vacate his post as caretaker of Homunculus Castle.

INTERNATIONAL NEWS AND POLITICS REPORT: Robbie Cox slams Sweet Jesus, says he's a political disgrace, says he does not deserve to be in the Superhero Hall of Fame. To sign the petition to have him removed, CLICK HERE.

50.

Interview with a Caucasian landowner, pt. 4: "At the Hospital"

(WARNING: This interview series is unedited. Anyone possibly offended by a melanin deficient WASP should stock up on Band-Aids and hide behind the nearest fire hydrant.)

INTERVIEWER: How are you the one who made it through this without needing a neck brace and who's going to pay my doctor bills?

CAUCASION LANDOWNER: It was my boat, it was the lake by my house, it was my day off work.

I: Hope she was worth it.

CL: She wasn't.

I: For the record, what was it again she said to you at the crash site?

CL: She said I'll sue your ass. And she walked it off and left me to die.

I: If I hadn't dragged you out of the flames.

CL: Hey, that's not the kind of attitude the nurse says I can deal with right now.

I: What are your thoughts on single issue voting in a time of international conflict?

CL: I only vote my conscience when it pertains to my life.

I: True or false: there's no place for reckless behavior in a civilized nation.

CL: I'll settle for anywhere with a sports channel.

I: True of false: Sweet Jesus betrayed his people.

CL: The second you get the nurse back here to speed up my pain drip, I'll tell you all about it.

I: She's never coming back.

CL: There's your attitude again.

I: Not the way you treated her.

CL: How. How did I treat her?

I: You objectified her like you would a flank steak.

CL: Nurse! I need a pain drip over hear! Come on. Somebody. NURSE!

I: Told you she's never coming back.

CL: Hey, I'm getting real sick of you and your neck brace.

I: What about my attitude?

CL: I don't know but it must be a bitch talking with that on.

I: It is.

CL: Next question!

51.

POLITICAL OP-ED: How are we still talking about this Sweet Jesus situation? That's the real question the international news reports should be printing up. Big surprise Sweet Jesus miffed his role as castle caretaker. The guy's probably senile and downright confused. Behind all the headlines, the question is still begging an answer: why is everyone talking about this non-issue? It's obvious. There must be nothing else going on. Why else would this even be news unless this story was simply the best they've got? This is more proof than ever that the viruses are lame head colds, the terrorists are all talk, the natural disasters aren't coming after anybody anytime soon, and the aliens are all too busy with their own galaxies to even pay half a mind to us. The world ain't ending. That's my prediction.

As for Sweet Jesus, it's worth mentioning that he is looking good decked out in his old costume again. Never thought I'd see the day when he went full superhero in the London night (even if it was to get drunk, harass innocent ladies, and nearly plummet to his death). But come on everybody, give the poor luminary a break!

52.

School got canceled. An emergency warning was issued to make sure parents kept their kids as far away as possible from other kids. There were too many of them infected. Like rats in a plague, you don't want them piling up together dead and rotting in the gutters.

Infected! That's the one word you don't want to hear. Not in your community or in your schools! Not during an episode of eerie radio silence from the powers that be when everyone knows the world might end at any moment.

There was a brief write-up in the local paper about the epidemic, but nothing more. No television news coverage. Like it was actually no big deal. But school was canceled again for a second week. Then a third.

Killian sat back and watched. Roaming the streets, sitting atop chimneys, sitting atop church steeples, and even climbing to the roof of the damn school building, he sat back and took it all in.

53.

Robbie Cox leaned against the railing of Westminster Bridge. He didn't look at the Thames or at anything, really. Just off into the distance until it was cut short by some obstruction, like buildings, the sky, or a bird maybe.

Something was troubling the young champion. He hadn't shaved and his clothes weren't pressed. His iron-clad toughness had worn thin, down to about the level of an average person.

What is it, Robbie? What's gotten ya down, ya dope? Muscle tone not up to snuff, or what?

"I want to start taking action," he said to himself. "Does the world need me to save it or not?"

It was extra frustrating having this thought because he was starting to sound like all the others, and he knew it. At least they were right about one thing: politicians are superheroes and superheroes are supposed to save the world. That's just obvious, right?

At least, it all seemed obvious until Eleanor George stood him up for their cocktail date. That was half an hour ago. And it was the second time in a row he'd been stood up.

What was he doing in London, anyway? One cocktail after another between press conferences and fucking George only when she needed him to follow through with a job. A lame job, usually. The job of a prick or a mindless tough guy at best.

All this and the birds squawking over the ugly Thames. And the guys with the fake beards holding signs on the bridge. LIBERATE DUDEBUDDY. Probably as good a cause as any in these end times.

54.

The bearded guys with the signs watched Robbie Cox walk away. He walked toward the Houses of Parliament; soon he was out of sight.

The bearded guys next appeared in the back of a tourist bus. They attracted the attention of several middle-aged American tourists, each of whom mentally calculated the odds that these suspicious-looking characters were terrorists.

An average of the sum total of the odds was 9 out of 10. The only reason to believe they weren't terrorists was the fact that they were on a tourist bus. Since when do terrorists have fun?

Then again, if they were terrorists, then they could only be on the tourist bus for one reason: to further their terrorist plot. So, in all likelihood, not only were these characters terrorists, but there was nearly a 100% chance that this particular tourist bus was destined for some horrific devilry.

The bearded guys were next seen riding the Piccadilly line of the Underground. While aboard the train, they were watched closely by security officials. These officials calculated the probability of whether or not these otherwise harmless jokers were serious vis-à-vis the messages on their signs. LIB-ERATE DUDEBUDDY.

After a silent stroll through Covent Garden, the bearded guys posted up with their signs outside a nightclub. Not a moment later, Robbie Cox appeared. He glanced at the bearded guys as he walked by. His expression said, "I don't see you for a second. And even if I did, no way in hell I'd acknowledge that I see you, so why don't you and your stupid signs just get lost?"

55.

"I'm not here. You got that."

"You mean, you're not here with me."

"I'm not here. But if I were here, I wouldn't be here with you. Not by any stretch of the imagination."

"That's fine. I can't imagine you being here anyway."

"You've got two minutes."

"This is something you'll want to hear."

"Now minus ten seconds."

"Eleanor George," said Sweet Jesus, "Is—"

"Why should I even believe you?" Robbie Cox jumped in. "You just want to turn her against me—just like she turned against you. You're tactless, you know that?"

"She already turned against you. Long before she ever paid me any notice at all. She was turned against you from the beginning."

"What beginning?"

"From the moment you were elected."

"You have no idea about that."

"Kyle Rick-Jones went to visit Militant King X."

"What does he have to do with anything?"

"Let me explain," said Sweet Jesus, as sweetly as possible. "According to the news sources, he went rogue—he sold out politicians everywhere by trying to sell a deadly virus to a terrorist."

"Of course he did, the son of a bitch."

"What if that's not what happened? We only know what the news reported. All of those news outlets are owned by Eleanor George. What if Kyle Rick-Jones wasn't selling out politicians everywhere? What if he was actually following orders from Eleanor George?"

"That's absurd."

"Is it? Aside from you, Kyle Rick-Jones is the only other politician I can think of who blindly adheres to his contract as a superhero."

"Sweet Jesus, you've finally lost it."

"Hold on a minute. Before you walk out, I want you to watch this."

Sweet Jesus turned on a tablet and opened the video of Kyle Rick-Jones dying at the hands of the terrorists.

"You've seen this video?"

"Of course."

"Watch it again. In slow motion. Watch his lips…"

The video was zoomed in on Kyle's face. Robbie Cox scoffed at this ordeal and only slightly leaned forward to watch.

"Okay…"

"I didn't see it at first, either. Apparently no one did. But I had a suspicion. Watch it again."

Sweet Jesus played the video a second time. This time he spoke while the video played, filling in for Kyle's last words:

"Eleanor George. That bitch. She set me up. She set me up."

Robbie Cox sat back in his chair. "So what," he said. "What's that supposed to mean?"

"The man's dying words were an accusation that he was 'set up' by Eleanor George. If he knew he was dying, what motive could he possibly have to blame George?"

"The terrorists would have a motive."

"Perhaps. But then why did they release the video without sound? If they wanted to implicate George, they could have done so easily."

Sweet Jesus played the video again from the start. This time, Robbie Cox mouthed the words himself. "Eleanor George… She set me up."

"Fine," said Robbie. "But if Eleanor George wanted to throw Kyle Rick-Jones to the terrorists, no doubt she had her reasons to do so."

Sweet Jesus took a moment to glance out the door of their meeting room to make sure no one was listening. He returned to his seat with a nervous smile.

"Paranoid?" asked Robbie.

"The publicity has not been kind to me. For these past days I've been followed by reporters. And thanks to your petition to have me removed from the Superhero Hall of Fame, my political ruination is complete."

"Hence your desperate, wild theories—trying to bring Eleanor George down with you."

"No. I knew about Eleanor George's involvement before any of the negative press toward me came about. I wanted to confirm my suspicions. I wanted proof. That's why I spied on her. If I hadn't gotten caught, I would be in a much better position. And she, right now, would no doubt be in my place."

"Hah! Eleanor George would never be in your place, no matter what happened. She's not a politician. She's beyond public scrutiny!"

"Perhaps. But she's not beyond scrutiny from the politicians—her present and future contracts could all be in jeopardy."

"You truly are a disgrace to the political system. Inciting a breach of political contracts is a capital offense!"

"Would you like to know what I saw that night? Any guess who George was talking to when I peeked in her window?"

Sweet Jesus slid his tablet across the table. Robbie froze. He stared at the image on the tablet without giving any reacting. But slowly his jaw locked and his eyes bulged.

The image showed Eleanor George in her office, facing a large screen. On her screen, there was a man's face and shoulders. The man was blurry, since the angle of the picture was not right. But in the context of the situation, the picture was clear enough.

"Do you recognize that man?" asked Sweet Jesus.

"Yes."

"Then maybe you can explain why Eleanor George was hav-

ing an intimate conversation with Militant King X in her office...at night...in her lingerie!"

Robbie Cox didn't answer.

"Or..." said Sweet Jesus, leaning forward with both hands
on the table, "maybe you'd like me to tell you what they were
talking about?"

A dark cloud seemed to settle over Robbie Cox. "Okay, man,
tell me everything," he said, flexing so many muscles his face
twitched.

56.

Get ready kids for today's cartoons! All day nonstop so we
better get a move on! No dilly-dallying or delays, kids! That's
right, we expect full tuned-in, eyeballs not-blinking, sittin
back, candy-snackin attention from here on out! Ready? All
set? Okay! Cartoon specials, here we come!

Today, a phony superhero was attacked by another phony superhero in downtown Oakland, California. What a riot!
Here's the live footage of the epic battle:

[Live Footage]

Exclusive: Man skips work for six years; no one notices. Six
years! That's like the time it takes to voyage to a distant galaxy,
set up a new civilization, colonize a few other planets while
you're at it, and then come back and catch up on your taxes!
Whew! How many kids out there think they'd get noticed if
they were MIA from school for six minutes? But the real question is, what was this guy up to for six years?! We'll have that
story for you later today!

Now it's time for...Celebrity Secrets! Lillie Lyli reveals her
cleavage secret with throwback photos and great tips for all

you young ladies! And guys...just don't get too excited!

—Trending! Trending! Trending!—

Check out these revealing shots of Lillie Lyli in evening dress around town. Want to know how she gets this crazy-hot cleavage in every pic no matter what? Here's her secret! Just tape your boobs up with tape so they're super lifted. It's easy! But be sure when lifting your boobs, first wipe away any lotion or else it's like a slippery fest and no one wants that!

Now a message from Makeup Creams of the Gods!

57.

Killian rode his bike out to the edge of town and watched the construction crew set up a barricade across the southbound freeway. It was the last main road to be barricaded. Now the entire town was sealed in tight from the outside world. No getting in or out.

With the mystery virus spreading faster every day, it wouldn't be long before the place was more of a graveyard than a town. It would be a quarantined mass grave site. And no one beyond that southbound barricade would even know about it.

Sitting on his bike, Killian watched from a distance as one of the construction men suddenly bent over, at once coughing and gasping for breath. It was an early sign of the sickness. The man leaned heavily against the wheel of a bulldozer, shaking his head as though in confusion, trying to get some air into his lungs. Everyone nearby slowly backed away. As the man's coughing fit started up again, he covered his mouth and stumbled off down the road on wobbly legs. The rest of the crew watched him depart in silence.

In other times, you would expect the man to be heading off to see a doctor. But nearly all of the doctors had already been buried. Those that were left were too sick or too scared to do anything to help.

Nothing else to see here, Killian hopped back onto his bike and pedaled quickly toward his destination. Jenny's house.

A few days ago, the mayor of the town had sent out a notice: everyone with an infected person in their household must place a black ribbon on their front door. Since then, Killian had ridden by Jenny's house every day. So long as her door didn't have a ribbon on it, he could return home for the day with some sense of hope.

Riding through her neighborhood, he glanced at all the houses. Each day there were a few more black ribbons posted. All the houses leading up to Jenny's were still clear. That was a good sign.

Killian came to a slow stop on his bike. The street was perfectly still. It was like the whole world stood still. There with the tall shrubbery along the driveway, the patch of flowers, and the maple tree in the front yard, was Jenny's house. There next to the bird feeder and past the wind chimes, right on the front door, was a black ribbon.

There was one light on in the house. And that was Jenny's room.

58.

Killian stood outside the laboratory where Uncle Jon worked. His feet were firmly set, his arms at his sides, his shoulders square. He stood right out in the open. People walked by. Cars went in and out of the parking lot. Oddly, Killian felt like he had the whole place to himself.

He was thinking about that time when Ms. Buckingham got after him for writing Dudebuddy for all the answers on his quiz. That was wrong, he said to himself. She shouldn't have gotten after me. I was only telling the truth. She knows it's true. Everybody does.

Killian started for the entrance to the laboratory. Dudebuddy, he thought. Dudebuddy, Dudebuddy, Dudebuddy. And every time that name zipped through his mind, he felt its force, its weird sovereignty. He became empowered by it until he felt invincible, just like the guy in the terrycloth bathrobe.

"Act like you own the place," said a voice in the back of his mind as he walked into the building.

"Cool lobby," said Killian to himself. "Just the way I like it."

He ignored the receptionist at the big desk and went straight for the elevators. There were two of them. It was lunchtime, so both were busy. All the scientists coming and going looked similar in a way to Uncle Jon: lame nerds to the core. Not politician material, that was for sure. Not by a long shot. Killian wasn't intimidated even a bit.

"Don't be intimidated," said the voice in his mind.

"I'm not!" said Killian to himself, irritated because wasn't this self-evident, how obviously non-intimidated he was?

He went up the elevator with a few nerds holding sandwiches. During the quick trip up, they talked about their sandwiches and not about science. Killian wondered if they could be any lamer if they tried.

"Here with someone, buddy?" asked one of the scientists as they exited the elevator.

"No," said Killian, like he owned the place.

"Well, if you need something, the receptionist is located right by the front door, downstairs."

"I'm looking for my uncle."

"Who's your uncle?"

"Don't answer!" said the voice in Killian's mind. "Just ignore the stupid sandwich eater. Walk right past him. Push him over. Steal his sandwich!"

"Uncle Jon," said Killian.

"Jon...? Jon Gilbert?"

"Yeah."

"I'm afraid he's not here. He hasn't shown up to work the past week."

"Is he sick?"

"Could be. Or on vacation?"

"Okay."

"Sorry about that, buddy. Guess you'll have to check back in later."

"Can I see his desk?"

The scientist guy was silent for a moment, evidently considering this. Finally he said, "You know, come to think of it, we're not really supposed to have visitors up here. Sorry about that. Maybe when your uncle is here, he can show you around. But there are a lot of dangerous chemicals and things. No one's really allowed up here, as a kind of rule. Do you want to be a scientist?"

"Don't answer that! He's just patronizing you and do you look as lame as these idiots? No!" said the voice in Killian's mind. "Forget this loser. Kick his shins! Spit on his glasses!"

"Maybe," said Killian, politely. "I'm not sure."

He could see Uncle Jon's desk. It was just a few tables away, toward the middle of the lab. There was a computer and lab equipment. There was a desk with files inside. The computer probably had a password. Maybe the files were locked but maybe they weren't. Possibly there were notes written down someplace in plain sight. Possibly there were answers. It was worth a shot. Kick this guy in the shins and make a run for it. Punch him in the gut and run around stealing everyone's Erlenmeyer flasks.

Dudebuddy, Dudebuddy, Dudebuddy, thought Killian, as he took the elevator back down.

"Bummer!" said the voice, as if it were a joke.

Returning home, Killian had an uneasy feeling in his gut. He was more confused than ever.

59.

Charlie and Al squeezed themselves into bus seats right as the bus driver hollered back, "Okay, who tracked in the dog shit?!"

A few people checked the bottoms of their shoes, others just cowered in their seats, hoping to avoid suspicion.

"Among common people," said Charlie, "wonders never cease."

"To this bus driver," said Al, "it's possibly the worst offense—tracking dog shit into his bus. One can only imagine it's like a stranger putting their feet up on your furniture."

Al pointed down the aisle of the bus, "And this rubbery runway," he said, "is like his Persian rug."

"Everyone check your shoes!" yelled the bus driver. "We're not leaving till this bus is cleaned up!"

More people than before checked their shoes. Others, confident in themselves, turned and looking up and down the aisle with annoyance.

Charlie and Al were among those to look up and down the aisle, scowling at everyone.

"Yet, this is the bus driver's finest hour," said Al. "The one time he gets to exercise his authority."

Charlie didn't answer. His scowl had departed. Shifting away from the aisle, he hunkered down into his seat as though preparing for the long, tiresome ride ahead.

The bus driver was on the war path. His nose was working on all cylinders and his eyes were bulging.

"I do smell something off color," said Al, now making a sour face and turning up his nose.

"Keep your head down," Charlie hissed.

The bus driver was approaching.

"Charlie...?" said Al.

"Keep quiet!" said Charlie, crouching down further than ever.

"Think you can hide from me, huh?" the bus driver bellowed. He was standing right in front of the two monarch, staring hard at Charlie. "You think if you duck down and hide, this whole mess will clean itself up?"

Charlie looked at Al for help. Al, however, had gone pale and appeared incapable of breathing, let alone offering support.

"Yeah, I'm talking to you, you old clown in a cow suit—or cow in a clown suit. Whatever you are!"

"I've heard enough!" shouted Charlie, huffing with embarrassment but suddenly animated to the fullest. "Sir, I will strike you!"

"Come on and get your fat arse up, you momma pig!"

That was too much for Charlie to take. He leapt up to throw a punch. But his lunge into battle didn't go quite as expected. Despite the incredible force of his leap, he budged only a few inches up from his seat, and there he got stuck, wedged partly jutting into the aisle.

"Oh no you don't," said bus driver like a scolding parent, "you're not going to get stuck in your seat with shit all over your shoes. Not on my bus!"

While Charlie swatted with hands and fists, the bus driver grabbed hold of Charlie by the shoulder and tugged. Al, wishing to escape this situation however possible, leaned against Charlie's girth and pushed from the other side.

"I'll strike you!" yelled Charlie wildly. "I'll strike you!"

The people on the bus cheered, but mostly for the bus driver.

It wasn't until half an hour later that the bus finally departed from the station. Charlie and Al stood there, watching it pull away.

"You know what, Al?" said Charlie, obsessively wiping the bottoms of his shoes on the grass. "I think that was the wrong bus anyway."

"You sure? I'm pretty turned around."

"I'm fairly positive."

"A drink, then? I could sure use a drink."

"All this traveling and we haven't found anyone who needs a king."

"Well, it's not like we're selling dental floss. A kingship is a high-priced commodity! All you need is to sell one and you're set for life!"

"That's what we thought before."

"True."

But right now I have bigger concerns. The smell of shit won't wipe off!"

60.

After his visit with Robbie Cox, Sweet Jesus fled London. He returned under cover to his home—not to Homunculus Castle, but to Arkansas. Back to his rustic place of birth. Right about where it rains the most in the Ozarks. Where it's shadowy and moldy and it's okay to not care about politics. When the world ends, if there's one place that doesn't hear about it, it'll be Sweet Jesus's home town in Arkansas.

It wasn't much of a town. Just some spread out shacks in the hills with one road along the way that had a gas station, a mini mart, an old bar, and not much else.

The rain was coming down. Shoulders slumped, Sweet Jesus walked into the bar. It was early afternoon. There were a few guys seated at the bar, but Sweet Jesus didn't pay them any attention. He just took a seat and wondered if he'd later regret drinking this early in the day.

"Beer?" asked he bartender.

"Yeah, alright," said Sweet Jesus.

While paying for the beer, he cleared his throat and tried to summon the remnants of his local accent. "You know if there's any property for sale around here?" he asked.

"What kinda property?"

"Anyplace with four walls and a bit of seclusion, you know."

"Oh yeah?"

Sweet Jesus thought for a moment. Then nodded, "Yeah."

"I'll keep an eye out for that."

"Thank you. Much appreciated."

"Heh, heh," the bartender laughed.

Sweet Jesus stared at his beer and thought about asking for water. He also thought about what to do next. If he stayed in Arkansas, would he lose his will to care about politics? Or would it haunt him forever? His reflections were interrupted when one of the guys at the bar came over. Without any introductions, the guy leaned right next to Sweet Jesus and slapped down a postcard.

"What do you think about this?" the guy asked.

Sweet Jesus glanced at the card. After a pause, he picked it up just to be polite. It wasn't a postcard after all; it was an advertisement for a bikini rodeo show in Little Rock. The front picture showed a girl riding a bull right as the bull's hind legs flailed in a ferocious buck. The girl held a cowboy hat over her head in one hand while holding onto the bull with the other. The side view of her breasts showed them to be full and excellent, covered just barely with a red bikini. Probably in the next instant after the picture was taken either her top fell off or she went head over heals right on her ass. Probably both.

"Down in Little Rock tonight," the guy said. "Everyone's gonna be there."

Sweet Jesus handed the card back. "I'm afraid I'm too old for that kind of thing."

"Keep it," said the guy, walking away.

It was only then that Sweet Jesus noticed the guy's strange clothes. He was wearing sandals and a terrycloth bathrobe. In Arkansas in a bar in the middle of the day? Now stepping out into the rain? On his way to a bikini rodeo show?

"You know I got an extra space out back here with room

enough for a cot," said the bartender. "If you're okay living with some chickens."

Sweet Jesus raised his beer in response. He took a long drink.

61.

Years ago on everyone's television screens but also in their hearts, the whole world came together to celebrate Sweet Jesus walking up on a stage, giving a speech, and getting inducted into the Superhero Hall of Fame. If it wasn't for him, the world would have ended at least a dozen times in half as many years.

"The world won't end today," he said in his speech, "not unless I talk too long and everyone dies in the end from sheer boredom." Something like that. Everyone laughed and laughed. What a champion! And good-natured, too!

But that was far away and long ago. Times were different now. The world might end at any moment, and no one even seemed to mind.

Perhaps I should mind a hell of a lot more myself, Sweet Jesus thought. But, oddly, he didn't.

He was standing outside a desolate warehouse on the outskirts of Little Rock. There weren't any markers on the warehouse, but the address spray-painted on the curb indicated that this was the right place. Sweet Jesus double-checked the flyer for the bikini rodeo show. Yep, this was the place.

The entrance to the warehouse was a heavy metal door. Just like the side entrance to Homunculus Castle. Suddenly feeling right at home, Sweet Jesus pushed his way inside.

"Stop," said a man immediately upon entering. The man—

apparently the bouncer—thrust something into Sweet Jesus's hands. "Put this on," he said.

It was so dark that Sweet Jesus couldn't tell what he'd been given. What was it, a stuffed animal? The thing slowly unfolded until it took on the shape of some sort of long garment. After finding the sleeves, Sweet Jesus realized that it was a pillowy bathrobe.

"You can undress around the corner," said the bouncer. "There's a place to hang your clothes. Then put that on."

Sweet Jesus nodded. He was already too deeply invested in this odd night in Little Rock to question this detail about the dress code.

While changing his clothes, he shut his eyes as they adjusted to the darkness. Was this place as creepy as it seemed? It had been a long time since he had been to any sort of nightclub in Arkansas. Opening his eyes, he glared down a long corridor that only vaguely hinted at a light source coming from under a door some distance away.

The robe fit great. So that was something. It was a downgrade in style for sure. It was slovenly and musty smelling. But somehow it felt just right—like the cape that complements the mask that inspires all the superpowers.

Who has ever heard of superpowers from a bathrobe?

Then he remembered the guy from earlier. The guy with the flyer. He'd also been wearing a bathrobe. Maybe it was a new trend. An Arkansas thing.

The cement floor was stone cold under bare feet. He made his way slowly down the corridor, still not able to see much of anything. But there were definitely sounds coming from beyond that door up ahead...

He started to picture girls. Lots of them in next to no clothes. Like the girl on the flyer. Her top loose on her breasts. About to fall off. Skinny young girls. Serving alcohol and riding bulls. He pictured bright flashing lights and everyone having a good time. Approaching the door at the end of the hall, he could almost hear the music blaring as the first girl stepped into the ring. He could almost hear the wild cheers of the cowboys, going crazy to see what might happen next.

The door swung right open—right into the huge expanse of the warehouse. Most of the space was lost in absolute darkness. Only the nearest corner was lit with florescent lights hanging over an unusual scene, which included a bar, a few tables, a few couches, an old piano, and a makeshift DJ booth. Occupying this scene, there were at least a dozen guys all wearing terrycloth bathrobes. There was no sign of half naked girls riding bulls.

One of the robed guys came forward holding a drink in hand. "Sweet Jesus!" said the guy with cheer and warmth, "glad you could make it. Come on over. Join us!"

62.

This chapter was supposed to be a political speech by Robby Cox about food labels for factory chickens. But the speech never happened. Robbie Cox was having a personal crisis and spent the day swimming with sharks and at one point swam to the third deepest underwater cavern on Earth to see if he could scare up a sea monster or two to fight. Finding none, he just stayed down there a while and held his breath until it hurt.

While he's still down there waiting for his lungs to burst,

here are a few alternate ideas for this chapter:

A political speech by Pliny the Younger about provincial governors taking bribes without first consulting an oracle.

A political speech by Benjamin Franklin in which he offers one thousand and one examples of his aphorism, "He that is good for making excuses is seldom good for anything else."

We could alternatively pull out a few random titles from The Trove of Anonymous Political Speeches Etc. Here are some.

"Upon Stabbing the Downtrodden in the Back on Your Way to the Bank."

"Dos and Don'ts for Gaining Lifelong Supporters, Vol. 1: Namedropping at the Country Club."

"Vol. 2: Soliciting Votes at the Striptease Show."

And here we have "The Collected Speech Templates for Politicians," which includes everything from "The Template Speech for After You Have Just Saved the World" to "The Template Speech for After the World Has Just Ended."

63.

It was all fun and games up until very recently. Now it's like open hunting season around here. The higher-ups are going through serious re-orgs. Just a minute ago one of the managing editors got canned, which really knocked the wind out of us copyeditors. We're staggering, demoralized from the blow. Heads down and typing away. Job security a thing of the past!

Right this second, brusque officials in the break room. Going through old coffee grounds looking for clues. Rummaging through lunch pails hoping for signs from the heavens.

They've already circled our cubicles. That means next they'll be horsing around in our email accounts. There's no respecting privacy for these guys. They'll know what we know, you bet your ass. That's not exactly what I mean but look. Don't have time to get all my expressions right. Just typing with head down.

Typos don't spell Armageddon. Nor most grammar fails. At a time like this, it's a matter of letting the fingers fly. No looking back.

What's so godawful important they've found in the ancient documents? If you ask me, it's still a matter of what they haven't found.

But there is this. One of the ancient documents (so old you'd never believe it) turned out to be a political type of flyer with the message on it translated as close as possible to read two words: "Liberate Dudebuddy."

Liberate. Verb. To set (someone) free from a situation, especially imprisonment or slavery.

Dudebuddy. Noun. Mysterious figurehead of the Dudebuddy Liberation Front (again according to our memory of childhood comics—oddly useful resources, it would seem) and possibly an imprisoned leader of Dudebuddy Nation.

Speculations abound. Okay, so what?

64

A call came for Eleanor George when she was right between thick slabs of meetings. Busy day. But she had to answer. It was her advisor for international media calling. He of all people knew what a busy day looked like.

"There's a town in America," he said, "where a lot of people are getting sick and dying. The local physicians have never seen anything like it. And every time they try to treat it, they catch it themselves. Schools have been shut down for three weeks. It's estimated that 65% of the town is infected. Local officials have just put a quarantine over the town."

"Send a memo. I'll look it over," said Eleanor.

"We have to report on something. It's been almost six months since the world leaders' conference and none of your news outlets have covered a single story relating to the growing threats."

"You're sure it's not Erectalphlegm Syndrome?"

"It's worse."

"Send me a memo."

"Can we report on it?"

"We've reported on too much already. From now on, uplifting stories only. Something for the whole family to watch."

"Everyone in this town is dying."

"Send me a memo." With that, she hung up just in time for her next meeting, re: Should daytime television be sexier? If so, how and how much?

65.

Jenny wasn't just any girl. Not to Killian. If she was the subject matter of a quiz, he'd ace it every time.

How tall was she? She was kinda short, just the right height, thought Killian.

What color was her hair? It was dark brown but also golden in the way it always seemed to catch the sunlight, even on a cloudy day.

What's one word to describe her smile, her laugh, and the glimmer in her eye all at the same time? Since there's no right or wrong answer for this one, a few options could be: cute, awesome, the best, and perfect if you ask me.

What's she like when she's running a high fever, her skin is broken out in red blotches, and she's lost her voice after getting infected with the latest epidemic? She's not herself. It's not good. It can't be happening. Not to Jenny.

66.

Interview with a Caucasian landowner, pt. 5: "At the Steakhouse" (WARNING: This interview series is unedited. All those unaccustomed to a privileged worldview should look away. Shield your eyes. Wear a blindfold and stick your head in the ground.)

INTERVIEWER: Have you ever considered vegetarianism as a healthy lifestyle alternative?

CAUCASION LANDOWNER: Let me tell you something. Practically everything I do is vegetarian. When I'm walkin' down the street, it's vegetarian. When I hit up the gym, it's vegetarian. When I'm shootin' some pool, drinkin' beers, and checkin' out some babes, it's vegetarian. But sometimes you've just got to break that cycle and enjoy a bloody-ass cut of beef.

I: Does your choice of eating animal flesh have any bearing on your decisions when you go to the polls?

CL: Sure, that's part of my vegetarian lifestyle. I like to keep my voting time strictly vegetarian. Not to say I wouldn't eat a damn burger at a voting booth, because I would. I just mean I haven't up to now, this moment.

I: How do you think that look you just gave that waitress makes her feel?

CL: Ah you saw her too, yeah? Wow! I'd tap that!

I: Yeah, I'm sure you would.

CL: Like to know where I can find some of that on the menu.

I: Which do you consider more likely: life itself ceasing to exist from a virus spread from either a) consumption of animal flesh, or b) sexual activity.

CL: Hm...I'd say probably fuckin'. Seems most likely like something you'd catch from fuckin' would get us first. It's the more reasonable option. That which bringeth life causes it to all go to shit in the end. Heh!

I: For the record, why don't you tell us why tonight you're celebrating.

CL: She's coming back around again.

I: You're celebrating tonight because...

CL: Excuse me, beautiful.

I: Tough luck.

CL: She just didn't hear. It's loud.

I: Uh-huh. But tonight's a night of celebration, you were saying earlier.

CL: Hell yeah it is. Because I'm a champion and I'm gonna kick everyone's asses in court!

I: Because you're a champion and you're going to kick everyone's asses in court. And you haven't considered hiring a lawyer?

CL: Naw, I got this easy, bud.

I: Not for the criminal or the civil charges?

CL: It was my boat, it was the lake by my house, it was my day off work.

I: When you're rotting in jail, in debt up to you neck with civil liabilities, will you regret the actions you've taken?

CL: Hold that dumbass thought a sec while I go and take a piss.

67.

INTERNATIONAL NEWS AND POLITICS REPORT: Robbie Cox fails to show at crucial food labeling talks. The contentious issue of what's to be done with labelling factory chicken legs and wings remains unresolved.

INTERNATIONAL NEWS AND POLITICS REPORT: Sweet Jesus has vanished in the aftermath of the Eleanor George spying scandal. His removal from the Superhero Hall of Fame is still pending.

INTERNATIONAL NEWS AND POLITICS REPORT: Militant King X declares war on everyone and everything. In a BREAKING video broadcast, he threatens widespread release of the dreaded Erectalphlegm Syndrome. Adult and child penis-owners everywhere are advised to remain on high alert for any unusual secretion activities.

68.

"If I'm going to destroy ze world, I will do it on ze terms zat are my own." (This was a secret communication.)

"Don't get ahead of yourself," (replied the secret respondent) "you're not destroying the world; you're only killing everyone on it."

"A technicality!"

"And you won't get very far along destroying anything without my authority."

"You need me!"

"No. I need the virus that I handed to you on a silver platter. I'm relying on you to carry out a course of action. If you fail, I can rely on someone else."

"It's my terms or no terms! You can take ze birus back!"

"Let's not get carried away. Fine. What are your terms?"

"I want to habe some fun. Zat is for a start."

"Of course."

"I want to be in ze spotlight."

"Noted. And hasn't that been happening?"

"I want an island all to my own wiz an unlimited subbly of ze rum of ze island nations."

"We can discuss that."

"Oh! And I want to defeat my ribal, causing him a slow and bainful dez, killing him wiz my own bare hands, in front of a libe audience."

"And who might that be?"

"You know who."

69.

Robbie Cox took the long elevator ride up to Eleanor George's London office. He thought about Sweet Jesus climbing all this way up the side of the building. That seemed like a pretty good idea. Why hadn't he thought of it first?

In his mind, he played the scene as a cartoon news broadcast: Robbie Cox! The world's best-loved superhero! On his way to visit the almighty Eleanor George. Will he take the elevator? No way! He'll scale the building hand over hand. No sweat! Wow, look at him go!

The elevator doors slid open. Clearing his throat, Robbie Cox stepped into the top-floor lobby.

Her door was shut. Knocking, Robbie could just see the news reports tomorrow announcing: Robbie Cox, that lousy excuse for a superhero—and everyone knows it!—just got his contract terminated! That's right, Eleanor George finally gave him the boot! Wow, how did this take so long?! It's about time!

Why else could she be calling him up here at such a last moment's notice. After she'd bailed on their last half-a-dozen-or-so dates!

"Get ready, Robbie old boy," he told himself, "—get ready to beg."

70.

Eleanor George was waiting with champagne. She had also prepared fruit tarts. Classical music played in the background. Just like the sounds of the triumphs of flowers blossoming on the hill-tops. Hell of a way to greet somebody with his head on the chopping block, thought Robbie Cox as he accepted a champagne flute.

"Do you believe in The End Times, Robbie?"

"Not a fan, but believe? Sure."

"You're more of a champion for the moment, I know."

"If there are such things as destructive forces, I like to think about how to stop them."

"I'll tell you a secret."

"I'm open to that."

"I don't believe in The End Times."

"What? Hmmm. Is that a kind of optimism?"

"I've never believed."

"So there's just eternity, plain and simple?"

"This champagne, this fruit tart, and everything else with it."

"I'm surprised at you."

"Oh? How so?" Eleanor smiled, her first sign of possibly flirting.

"You have to admit," said Robbie, "you have a very particular relationship with The End Times. Given your position in terms of saving the world."

"That's just politics, which is so much more complicated."

"Marketing... Contracts..." Robbie shook his head, understanding completely. He finished his champagne and quickly got more. This conversation wasn't making him feel any more secure in his situation.

The word contracts hung in the air as though it had been shouted, as though it left a ringing sound. Robbie couldn't think of anything to say next. So the word just stayed there, ringing away.

"I need your help, Robbie," Eleanor said at last.

"I'm your man."

"There is the list of all the ways the world might end at any moment."

"You said we were going to wait on that. That it didn't matter..."

"Well, we've waited long enough. The time is now ripe. Anxiety levels around the world have peaked, for all demographics. For the first time in decades, people are really starting to believe that the world might come to an end at any moment. Now is the time to take advantage."

"So that's why I'm here—to help you save the world?"

"Yes. I know that's what you wanted."

"I'm ready."

"That's what I like to hear."

Robbie gulped down his champagne. "Let's do it," he said, flexing.

"First we need to talk about our strategy."

"Big time."

"More champagne?"

"Fill her up."

"We'll begin," she said, emptying the bottle, "with Militant King X."

71.

(Another secret communication. This time in the early morning at a zoo. Black crows squawking. What were they saying. Dumb, dumb people? This cool sky is all mine, mine, mine? They circled around and perched in the trees. Watching like spies.)

"You're a double crossing devil woman! Zat's why I love you!"

"No," (replied the secret respondent) "a utilitarian."

"Media beeble are my new faborite beeble."

"Do you always dress this way?"

"One day you'll understand."

"Don't expect me to."

"Four brilliant words I gibe to you. One size fits all."

"I still have my doubts, but okay."

"Now, we have ze terms of ze blan."

"But I still need the map. You have a map for me."

"Ah, yes. Ze mab. Here it is. Simble. Easy to read. It is ze only mab of ze desert wiz details like zis. But it cannot get into ze wrong hands! You understand? He-he!"

"Of course."

"And so, we hab our blan, and we boz get what we want. Yes?"

(Silence on the part of the secret respondent as she looked

off at the rolling hills of fake jungle scenery. Over the peak of the most distant hill, the first rays of the morning sunlight appeared. Wake up, wake up, wake up, said the rays to the world.)

"Why did you want to meet at a zoo," (asked the secret respondent).

"Because," (said the secret personage, now with a wild grin on his face) "I wanted to see ze snakes."

72.

First day in the big city, Charlie and Al were all set to conquer the assorted tourist traps.

"Time to live it up, Al," said Charlie. "Time to loosen up the old codpiece."

"I want to go see the—"

"No you don't."

"I was just going to say the—"

"Don't even say it."

"The cathedral."

Charlie stopped, grabbed Al by the shoulder, pushed him up against a stone building, tossed his cigar on the sidewalk, cursed.

"Listen buddy," said Charlie, "we're here for the tourist traps, the fine dining, the beautiful ladies, and the luxury hotel suites. We're not here to reevaluate our spiritual place in this world."

"I just want to go see the building."

"Oh, so you're some big fan of architecture now?"

"I had a cathedral built for me once," said Al, timidly.

"Well, so did I."

They continued walking, silently wondering all about the

other's cathedral. By the end of the block, they had both become so jealous that it would almost certainly be sometime before either of them would have anything pleasant to say.

Eventually they were completely lost, wandering further and further away from all the good tourist spots. They kept turning down the wrong streets, until every possible street seemed wrong.

"Here you go," said Charlie. "You got your wish."

They were walking right up to a church. It was a brick, half-mast-steeple sort of church. Not exactly St. Paul's.

"I just really want a cup of tea," said Al, turning his eyes to the ground.

"Oh yeah? No ladies, opera tickets, penthouse suites?"

"No," said Al, quietly sulking.

"Okay, buddy," said Charlie, taking his royal companion around the shoulder, leading him away from the church. "Let's go get you a cup of tea."

73.

POLITICAL OP-ED: You know what I think happened to Sweet Jesus? I'll tell you. He's taking a nice vacation. He's in the Bahamas. Either that or Hawaii. Maybe Miami or even Rio de Janeiro. That's where'd I'd be. Think about it. He's retirement age. Not only that, he's technically been retired for the past decade. All this drama that's happened recently—he doesn't need any of that!

I keep writing about this even though I don't particularly care that much about Sweet Jesus. It's just that there's nothing else happening. Everything is doing great and the future is looking up, up, up. This is the best shape the world has ever been in—and I mean ever. Let's not forget that.

Who's given thanks for their local superhero today? I have. But I might just do it again. I feel so grateful. Who's with me?

74.

The warehouse in Arkansas may not have had bikini girls riding bulls, but it did have the ways and the means to show a guy a good time. It had a decked-out bar. It had a piano, a DJ booth, and a pool table. But more than any of that, it had the promise of tangible freedom. The promise of being able to take a step back—back to a place where you can safely re-examine your standing in the world, re-examine the world itself, burrow deep underground, and ultimately resurface somewhere completely new and unexpected—free and re-imagined.

(Forget about the bikini girls. Just pretend that was never a possibility. If you're hung up on the bikini girls, you'll miss the true significance of the Arkansas warehouse. Fair warning!)

"Ready for round 500, Mike?" asked Clint, loosening the belt on his bathrobe. Mike was the name the bathrobe guys had given Sweet Jesus. He didn't look like a Mike, but that was beside the point. Somehow it fit.

"Round 500?" asked Mike. "Feels like 5 million." He was slurring his words and wobbly on his feet. He was so drunk, he couldn't say where he was or how he'd gotten here. He was so drunk, he took it for granted that his name was Mike and all he could do was keep on losing terribly at pool.

"Sure, but who's counting?" Clint said, racking up the balls.

"Hey Mike," said a guy named Richie. "Why don't you tell us more stories about your favorite pastime?"

"Saving the world?" Mike asked, not sure why he'd said that.

"No—ha, ha! fishing crawdads!"

"Also..." said Clint, jabbing Mike in the ribs, horsing around like a longtime friend. "I'd love to hear more about your secret ambition in life."

"To be a superhero?"

"No, no! To start a bluegrass band!"

Mike held up a finger, weakly, as if to say, "One moment." Then he tottered off into a corner where he puked into a bucket. It was his puking corner. The only place around here he really felt at home.

"Where am I?" he asked himself as he leaned his head against the side of a cold cement wall. "What am I doing here?"

These questions suddenly seemed so dreary, as if he'd already asked them a hundred times. Only to arrive at the answer: what does it matter?

He really only seemed to remember one thing. Bikini girls riding mechanical bulls. With a certain mental effort, he could almost picture it. Hot southern babes in cutoff jean shorts and brightly-colored bikini tops. Straddling ugly, angry bulls. Waving over their heads frayed cowboy hats. Always mid-buck—never falling off. Their breasts always full and glistening, just about ready to spill out and bounce free.

"To spill out and bounce free," he muttered, vomit dripping off his bottom lip.

This scene in his mind was inevitably interrupted by the more present, more real memory of Clint's voice saying, "Forget about the bikini girls. Just pretend that was never a possibility. If you're hung up on the bikini girls, you'll miss the true significance of the Arkansas warehouse. Fair warning!"

Back at the pool table, Clint was just squaring off for the break.

"Hey there, partner," said Richie, "how about another drink?"

"Well, sure," said Mike. "Why not?"

75.

Killian stood in the shade of a stumpy oak tree, a few paces removed from the others. He had come to develop the habits recently of a moody detective—the type hired by people who like being grunted at while given sad, sidelong, suspicious glances.

He was also the only child at the funeral service. Everyone else was past the age of having secret under cover missions. That's what Killian had. No paycheck attached, either. Nothing anyone around here could understand.

Over the past week, thirty-seven people had died in the town. The funeral service was being held to commemorate their lives. This had become a weekly event. The weekly funeral service for five to fifty or so townspeople. Like the end of the world, slowly, one handful of townspeople at a time.

Killian kept his distance during the entire service. He scarcely moved. Each time the breeze rustled his hair, he tried hard not to blink.

Jenny was up there. Lying dressed up and painted to look nice. In a coffin, cold and still.

If only he had ever really spoken to her. Really gotten to know her. To be with her alone and tell her everything. How she was the perfect girl. The girl he thought about all the time. And how that meant something.

Then things would have been different. Somehow this never would have happened. He should have spoken to her when he had the chance. But it was too late.

Killian figured he'd wait until the funeral was over. Until everyone had gone. Then his detective work could really begin. He'd get to the bottom of this.

The breeze was growing stronger. Something about that breeze was simply unbearable. It wouldn't leave him alone. Finally he had to blink against it, and a tear fell. Two tears. They slid all the way down his cheeks, all the way to his chin. He blinked again, hard. The tears kept coming. Even through his closed, pressed-together eyelids. But he wouldn't wipe away his tears. No way.

76.

Leaving the cemetery, Killian kicked at the gravel along the path and picked up sticks to break over his knee and throw. Suddenly he slipped on the gravel. His legs flew up and he fell straight back. He came to his feet slowly, his hands scraped raw. As he wiped the dirt off his pants, he also rubbed his face against the crook of his arm, finally wiping away the stream of tears.

Then he froze. Looking up the path, the parking lot was a short distance ahead. There, leaning against a familiar truck, was Uncle Jon. His arms were crossed and he was staring right at Killian.

This wasn't how it was supposed to happen. Killian was supposed to track him down, not the other way around. Detectives weren't supposed to be taken by surprise.

"Hi-ya, Killian," said Uncle Jon.

Killian coughed and forced his cheeks to pull slightly into a smile. He felt like a cross between a plucked chicken and a deer in the headlights. Unable to find any words, he tried to yawn and to stretch his arms, but that just made his clumsiness even more of a spectacle.

"How was the funeral?" asked Uncle Jon, taking a few steps forward to meet Killian at the edge of the parking lot.

Killian shrugged.

"Where's your bike?"

"I walked," Killian said finally, clearing his throat.

"All this way?"

"Yeah, got a flat."

"Uh-oh."

Killian's legs felt shaky. He couldn't look Uncle Jon in the face.

"Here," said Uncle Jon, motioning toward his truck. "Hop in. I want to show you something."

"What?"

"I want you to meet someone."

"Who?"

"Back at my place."

Killian slumped into the passenger seat. He willed himself back into detective mode. Check out all these clues, he thought. Clues like it's the moment everything starts to come together. Like the coffee mug smelling up the whole truck cab with the smell of black coffee. That was something. Also the way they were driving so fast—it was definitely faster than might be considered necessary, so whatever was back at Uncle Jon's place, it was likely something that couldn't wait.

Like a type of bug that only lives a few hours?

Or a chemical that turns into another color after a certain time and goes bad?

Maybe it was a surprise and Uncle Jon was just excited about it?

As he sat there enduring the stiff silence with his uncle, Killian became suddenly aware that perhaps this wasn't detective mode after all. Instead, just possibly, it was something else altogether. Revenge mode? Yeah, maybe that was it. Revenge mode, thought Killian, saying it over and over, until it sounded like applesauce, or hot sale item, or some other ultra-normal thing.

But revenge mode—it still made sense. And with luck, it was possibly not oh-so-different from save the world mode.

"Almost there," said Uncle Jon. He looked over at Killian and saw his bleeding hands. "Ouch," he said. "I'll have to get you a bandage for that."

"No," said Killian. He folded his hands on his lap. "It's okay."

"You sure? Looks like it hurts."

"Yeah," said Killian, not really wanting to admit that it throbbed so much he almost didn't care what happened next.

77.

Okay again we think we may have found something, but who knows—of all things, this could really be a serious rabbit hole to God knows where. Got to be ready for anything at this point.

Hey, it's the copyeditors here. This time together in a garage after work hours with a case of beer to keep us refreshed. It has come to this: searching through our old comic books. Secretly it was something, I think, we all wanted. Rather than keeping up with our petty denials of the truth, we came out and confessed to keeping trunks, chests, or boxes full of comic books from our long gone school days.

We had the comic books laid out all over the place. Our task was a simple one. Simpler than copyediting a politician's grocery list, which of course is a thing and not just something we all joke about. We were to dig deep for anything referring to Dudebuddy, Dudebuddy Nation, and the Dudebuddy Liberation Front (DLF).

Only with these references in our pockets will we ever have a chance of understanding the ancient documents. The ones right under our noses, being picked apart sometimes right on the other side of our very cubicles.

"Jeez, some of these female characters really sure do let it all hang out," said one of the copyeditors, pouring over comic books on his hands and knees in the garage.

"Yeah," said another copyeditor, "like check out Alalia, Secretary of Interstellar Space Stations." He held up a picture. "I mean, come on, wow, huh?"

"Boy, do I remember this one: Katilexy, commander of that badass alien race, you know?"

"Come on, guys, take it easy," said one of the female copyeditors, rolling her eyes.

Our search carried on. Late into the night and many cases of beer later. A reference here, a character alluding to something referential there. Slowly, just possibly, it was all beginning to add up.

78.

Killian hadn't been back to Uncle Jon's place since that one time he'd been kidnapped and fell deathly ill. Ever since then, something had kept him away—even when he was on the hunt for Uncle Jon.

Now he knew why he had stayed away. As he followed his uncle through the front door, he knew for sure.

A rush of sensations nearly made him pass out right on the spot. His thoughts replayed old thoughts, like: You're sick as hell! You're going to die! It hurts so bad!

And he remembered how he'd just say horrible curses in his mind and wish for the worst to at least come soon, since that was all he could expect. But then Uncle Jon brought the cure. Right at the very last moment. Not a moment too soon or too late. Now that some time had passed, Killian's suspicions were stronger than ever. That Uncle Jon only possessed the cure because he also had the disease. In an Erlenmeyer flask. Someplace hidden away right here in this home.

"I want you to meet someone," said Uncle Jon.

"Okay," said Killian.

Suddenly there was an explosion of purple smoke. Killian jumped back at the sound, and for a moment he was blinded. But the smoke cleared quickly. And there stood a guy casually looking like he'd spent the last two days laughing at TV shows and drinking soda pop. It was the man from Killian's dreams—the man in the terrycloth bathrobe.

"I really like this purple smoke," said the guy. "Cool trick! I think I may just have to make this my regular mode of entry."

"This is the guy I've told you about," said Uncle Jon to Killian, "ever since you were little."

"We've met," said the guy, brushing off the last of the purple smoke, which twirled away and disappeared. "But never on a first name basis. We like to keep it hypnagogic. But hell—here's to concrete selloutery. I'm Meriwether."

He stuck out his hand. Killian shook it, not quite making eye contact.

"Meriwether?" said Uncle Jon.

"Sure," said Meriwether, "why not?"

"I guess I never—"

"Well, first names are just—you know. I almost prefer to keep it mysterious, but it's all the same! Alright—" he turned, motioning for them to follow.

Killian hesitated. Something didn't feel right about this. He glanced quickly around for a possible escape. Out the window, he caught a glimpse of two more guys in bathrobes; they were standing on the street corner holding signs that read: LIBERATE DUDEBUDDY.

Just then Uncle Jon grabbed Killian by the arm and dragged him along. The next moment, everything went dark.

79.

A desert scene at night.

Now the fate of the world is in my hands. Thought Robbie Cox. It was mostly his adrenaline talking. His adrenaline was his personal favorite announcer in terms of his thoughts. Among other dignifying turns of phrase, his adrenaline had been known to shout: The apocalypse has a great ass but I only dance with girls going places. He was about twelve years old when he shouted that. He began abusing the end of the world young like that.

It was dark under the open floodgate of the night sky. There's a particular ghostliness to the night's darkness when you're lost. It's like the night sky looks right past you—like the ghost is you.

Robbie Cox trudged along, one foot over the other, right into the heart of the most uncharted dunes in the desert. The wind whipped around; Robbie whipped it right back. He stomped on snakes, spit on spiders, and snubbed any blatantly suspicious shadows.

And finally he arrived to the point of thinking, so this is the place, huh. He was right on the fringe of Militant King X's secret compound. At least, that's where he was according to the instructions given to him by Eleanor George. He looked around at all the endless sameness of the dunes in the darkness. The fate of the world— etc., he thought again. He wondered what exactly might happen next.

"Who's that?" asked Killian.

"Don't you know?" said Uncle Jon, his tone unusually agitated.

"Is he—a bad guy?"

Uncle Jon grunted, shook his head.

"That's Robbie Cox," said Meriwether, the man in the terrycloth bathrobe. "He's a big-time politician."

"The superhero!" said Killian, remembering from his cartoons. "What's he doing?"

"Shh," Uncle Jon held up his hand as if expecting something dramatic to happen at any moment.

Nothing happened.

"He's having an internal struggle," said Meriwether.

"Oh..." said Killian, trying to understand.

They were standing on top of a sand dune less than ten paces from Robbie Cox. Somehow Robbie couldn't see or hear them. It was like they weren't really there. Except they were. The desert breeze felt like nothing Killian had ever quite experienced. And the sand underfoot wasn't any sort of trick, either. It was definitely the real sand of a real sand dune, surrounded by millions of others. It was all sand dunes and stars. Killian shivered; his spine tingled; he sunk a little deeper into the sand.

"He's on a mission to kill Militant King X," said Meriwether. "But right now he's having second thoughts. He senses that something's not right. He has a feeling that he may have been set up."

"What's going to happen?" asked Killian.

"Let's watch," said Meriwether.

Robbie got down on his hands and knees. He felt around in the sand as though he had dropped something. After a few minutes, he became visibly frustrated, like a kid trying to dig to the other side of the world, not completely sure where to start digging. According to his instructions, there was supposed to be a trapdoor right around here.

This must be it, he thought. A hard surface. He brushed away the last of the sand, revealing a small wooden door.

So far, so good, he thought. He'd had a few days to think up a backup plan, just in case Eleanor George was screwing him over, as Sweet Jesus had warned. His idea was to follow Eleanor's instructions only up to a point, and then to cleverly make a slight change of course so that he'd have the upper hand no matter what. He'd come up with all sorts of brilliant tactics, hundreds of them. But right here there was only one option. Just this trap door.

"Don't do it," said Killian. He immediately regretted speaking out loud.

"Shh!" warned Uncle Jon.

"There he goes," said Meriwether, narrating. "He's lifting the trap door. He's going inside."

80.

INTERNATIONAL NEWS AND POLITICS REPORT: Cartoon viewership hit record highs today and the numbers are expected to continue climbing. Analysts attribute the spike in viewership to the infamous plot of Militant King X, who poses the very real threat of unleashing Erectalphlegm Syndrome upon the masses at any moment.

81.

Eleanor George opened another champagne bottle. She was alone in her office. It was late at night and there were no lights except for the dim bulb of the lamp on her desk. She poured her champagne into a crystal flute and raised the drink in a toast to the screen she was watching, as though toasting in approval to the show on the screen. She took a sip and then watched Robbie Cox taking the ladder one step at a time down into the secret entrance to Militant King X's hideout.

"Yes, I see him now," she said. Her voice was stern and authoritative.

She was silent for a moment, watching with a scowl. On the screen, Robbie appeared at various angles during his descent as he came in and out of view of night-vision cameras. He showed up as an alien caricature of himself, green and out of focus.

Reaching the end of the ladder, he turned on a penlight to check for footing. It was only a short drop to solid ground.

Crouching at the bottom of the ladder, he shown his penlight down the long walls of the underground cave.

As though narrating, Eleanor explained, "His instructions tell him to walk half a mile straight, then take a left at the fork, and then take a few more turns, until he finds a—"

"He quick will find out zere's not a half a mile of straight," said a man's voice over a speaker. In contrast to Eleanor's British accent, the man's accent was distinctly Arabic. "Do you not know how long it takes to dig a foot of ze tunnel, woman?"

"Who's that?" asked Killian, standing by the window in Eleanor George's office.

"Shh!" said Uncle Jon.

"That's Militant King X," said Meriwether.

Killian nodded, vaguely drawing some connection to something he'd seen in cartoons. Uncle Jon almost opened his mouth to speak, but stopped himself.

"I only had the map you gave me," Eleanor was saying, "and it not only lacked a scale, it was sloppy in all respects, so forgive me if—"

"Ah, it's fine!" barked the man. "It's a maze under zere. All ze better if he does get lost."

"And there is no way of escape?"

"None. Zat full bortion of ze cabes hab been barricaded and ze entrance he used hab been already locked from ze surface. If he does not fall into ze snake bit, get attacked by ze scorbions, or—"

"I don't want him killed," said Eleanor. "That I made very clear."

"I only joke about ze snake bit. Ha, ha."

"Watch him. Don't let him escape and don't let him be killed."

"Yes, woman. Okay."

Eleanor sipped her drink, nodding approval as she watched Robbie Cox stumble in the darkness of the underground cave. "Good," she said.

82.

Eleanor shut off her computer, shuffled some papers on her desk, and turned around.

"Oh!" she said, startled by the unexpected company.

"Hey, El," said Meriwether, like an old friend.

"How long have you been here?"

"I'd like you to meet Dr. Jon Gilbert, one of our most successful operatives in America. And this is his nephew, Killian."

Eleanor acknowledged them with a blank expression. She looked them over, first Uncle Jon, then Killian, who stared back at her as though she were some kind of rare zoo exhibit.

"I know what you're thinking, El. You spend too much time in this godforsaken office. Let's go someplace with less London skyline. You can keep the champagne. What are you drinking, Kil?"

Sitting in steaming water up to his shoulders, squinting through incredible sunlight, Killian looked around in surprise. Everything was too bright. He had to close his eyes. Then he splashed his face with water. It was the best feeling. Like falling asleep for just an instant under the comfort of a liquid blanket. Wiping the water off his face and over his hair, Killian peaked at Eleanor George, an attractive, not-quite-past-her-prime woman now in a white swimsuit, reclining in a tile hot tub overlooking the endless baby blue of sky and ocean.

Meriwether, rosy-cheeked with hair newly wet and slicked-back, raised an arm to summon a young girl holding a tray of drinks. She was wearing a pink sash around her hips and a polka-dot bikini top. Her hair was pulled back. Not comprehending that she could be real, Killian couldn't take his eyes off her. Before he knew what was happening, she had turned to walk away, and he was holding a glistening cocktail with an umbrella and a slice of lime.

"Cheers," said Meriwether. "Welcome to Cancun."

"This is so tacky of you, Meriwether," said Eleanor. "And it's so bright here, I can hardly see a thing."

"That's just your comfort zone talking. But you can close your eyes if you want. Not much to see around here except paradise."

"Hm!" said Uncle Jon, putting on an exaggerated face of enjoyment. He was clearly out of his comfort zone, too.

Scowling, Eleanor turned to Uncle Jon. "And what exactly do you contribute?" she asked.

"I'm a scientist," he said, then stopped, apparently unsure what she wanted to hear.

"Hey!" said Killian. Meriwether had vanished without warning.

"Where did he—?" said Uncle Jon, squinting around the premises, from one group of bikini girls to another.

Eleanor George just sipped her drink, rolling her eyes at everything.

"Okay, I'm back," said Meriwether the next moment. "How long was I gone? Forget it. Okay, let's get this over with. By the way, I brought sunglasses." He handed them around.

"Now," he continued, "here's the upshot. The world has to end, and fast. That's coming from the place beyond politics—way beyond a place where anybody might have a say in the matter. Eleanor, you pretend like you know something about that, but you don't really; but that's okay.

"All three of you were chosen as envoys—chosen for your faithfulness but also for your positions and abilities in terms of bringing about the world's end. Killian, just so you know, in case you were wondering: you were to be the next great politician. You can't really do much to help the world end, since you're just a kid, but you've been particularly faithful; and since you were destined to be so important in this world, it was decided that you'd be allowed to come on board to the next one. In any case, your uncle insisted."

"And what exactly did Dr. Gilbert do?" asked Eleanor.

"Hah! This guy! I'd watch out for him! As you might know, El, we had a little contest, which Dr. Gilbert here won easily."

"Contest?" asked Killian.

"Yeah! Just something for fun advertised to geeky science communities. It was a contest to see who could create the deadliest virus—just in case anyone ever wanted to start a plague and kill off whole populations. Which of course is what we want to do."

"You mean," Eleanor said, "as a back-up plan to Erectal-phlegm Syndrome, which I personally undertook to harness and disseminate."

Uncle Jon smiled awkwardly.

"Back-up plan isn't quite how I'd put it," said Meriwether. "More like: another important weapon in a complex arsenal. Killing off a dominant species and destroying the plant Earth as much as possible on short notice is not as easy as launching one simple disease. Not to say Erectalphlegm Syndrome isn't my jam. It's a beauty. If you could end the world with something that stupid, I'd say hell yeah let's do it."

"So there's more?" asked Killian.

Eleanor flashed him a condescending look. She took a long drink of her champagne. It wasn't clear at this point whether she was sulking or drunk.

"Oh yes!" said Meriwether. "Lots of them! And Eleanor has done a fine job keeping them all secret. No good causing mass hysteria. In fact, that could lead to some challenges later on, spiritually speaking. Better to keep everyone oblivious, kill them off as slowly as possible leading up to the big event. Then pulverize the hell out of whatever's left in a sort of glorious celebration of destruction."

"Why don't you stop the world from ending?" asked Killian. He wasn't quite sure if his question made sense. But he had to ask it. Had he missed something? He looked up at his uncle, pleading for an answer—or any sign of good news.

Reaching a long arm out of the pool, Meriwether grabbed his robe, rustled around in the pockets, and pulled out a sheet of paper. Ignoring Killian, he held up the paper and said, "Remember this?"

"I believe you've already knocked your point home, Meriwether," said Eleanor. "That's really so unnecessary."

"Unnecessary but why not? I'm the public relations guy in the outfit. Or the angel of death, if you want to get morbid about it. In any case, you'll remember this… It's the list of this year's top things that could cause the world to end at any moment. It's the annual marketing ploy, that thing you use to give superheroes something to do. But this one isn't just a game. It's the genuine article. The recipe for the end of the world. Check it out! Here! Item number one: Erectalphlegm Syndrome! Eleanor, that's you! Item number two: mysterious giant virus rediscovered and reimagined. Dr. Gilbert, that's you! Hah!"

Meriwether leaned back his head to let out a great laugh when he disappeared again. The list was left behind, floating face down in the pool.

83.

POLITICAL OP-ED: Now I'm sure of it! Sweet Jesus is having a nice vacation, and Robbie Cox—I'll bet my lunch money—went to join him. This is all the more reason to believe that the world is in better shape than ever. The economy? Speaking from this author's vantage point—it's great! Look at me. I'm drinking on the job! Hell, I might even go home early today. News commentating in these times of opulence and whatever—it's a breeze!

84.

A flock of ravenous pigeons circled the high rise, looking for dumpsters to dive bomb. To the office workers inside the top stories of the high rise, it looked like they were all fighting with each other to get the best shots at shitting on the windows.

"Damn birds!" grumbled one of the office workers. "You believe in signs? That's an omen. A bad sign."

Al looked over at the grumbling office worker. He just looked at him for a few moments, slowly registering what had just been said, then looked out the window, then shrugged. Everyone was always grumbling around here. But who had time to grumble? Al, for one, had work to do.

Back home, Al had his dope-fiend buddy Charlie to care for. And there was no caring for anybody without the necessary cash-flow. In Al's case, that meant bi-monthly paychecks and the prospect of an annual bonus.

He had come down to nearly his last gemstone in his crown. Actually, he had six left. He counted them obsessively. But when you start out with an even 50, suddenly the plain, single-digit number six doesn't seem like so much. At this point, Al would rather start lopping off chunks of gold from the crown's God-given anatomy then rip out another gemstone. But even that was positively unthinkable so long as there were alternatives. And so it had come to this: honest employment.

Someone had to do it. And it sure as hell wasn't going to be Charlie. Ever since coming to the city, he had been doped up. That's what happens, isn't it? You come to the big city, you go out for a cup of tea, you meet some questionable company who shove dope down your throat with big promises of how good it'll be, and then, bam, you're hooked. It doesn't matter if you were a monarch for centuries and you've still got the promise of going places even at this point of your well-tread retirement years—it doesn't matter: it can happen to anyone.

By the end of his first week at work, Al had already started to get it about the pigeons.

"Damn birds!" he grumbled along with the chorus of grumbling office workers. "Their shit is ruining the only good thing left I've got going for my life: that view of the dumpster down below that I need so bad to visualize for what I'll fall into on that great day when I decide at long last to jump."

85.

Killian woke up slowly. He was in his own bed, and it was morning. He opened his eyes just enough to register these things. But then he closed them again and tried to focus on the memory of his dreams. There was one about being lost in the forest. The imagery wasn't at all sinister, but there was an undertone of things about to go wrong.

Stretching, Killian lifted himself up and made ready to hop out of bed. Just then his hand touched something on the edge of the bed: a sheet of paper. He picked it up. It was damp—soggy. Immediately Killian recognized the list from the pool in Cancun. The whole night's adventures flashed into his mind.

He sat up in bed, holding the paper in both hands. He read through the list. Then he stood up and walked over to the window. Outside, it was a normal day. No school, as usual. Nothing to do but to wait for the plague to come. But then what?

Killian read through the list again.

86.

TEN WAYS IN WHICH LIFE ON EARTH IS TO BE ANNIHILATED AT ANY MOMENT ACCORDING TO THE GRAND SCHEME.

1. Erectalphlegm Syndrome
2. Mysterious giant virus rediscovered and reimagined
3. Random asteroid impact
4. Global nuclear war
5. Artificial superintelligence turns against all biological life
6. Apocalyptic terrorist uprising
7. Rogue black hole
8. Particle accelerator disaster
9. Supervolcano eruption

10. Monster solar flare

87.

Interview with a Caucasian landowner, pt. 6: "On the Job" (WARNING: This interview series is unedited. Do you need some other diversion to get your mind off these evil things you're better off not reading? How about lawn bowling? Competitive yoga, we've been told, is another harmless option.)

INTERVIEWER: How long do you have to be on your knees like that?

CAUCASION LANDOWNER: Jesus, you make it sound like I suck cock for a living.

I: You enjoy construction?

CL: Ah, I don't really give a shit. You know I built my own house? The back part, anyway. The deck.

SITE MANAGER: Who's this chode?

CL: He's the interviewer. Show some respect, you jerkoff!

SM: Huh. Where's your hard hat, buddy? You stupid or something? Hard hat zone.

I: He said...

CL: Ha, ha! Told him it's safe. Ha, ha!

SM: Put this on.

I: Thanks.

CL: So what about that Adderoll?

SM: Same as always, bud. You have to go there to get it. It takes twenty-five minutes.

CL: You got twenty-five minutes?

I: Sure.

CL: I can drive.

SM (mocking): I can drive!

CL: What?

SM: You're drunk as shit, you chronic masturbator.

CL: Hey, you son of a bitch, I'm a Caucasian landowner.

SM: Yeah, and before that you were a Sudanese street urchin. Just pulling wallets and shit. Just sniffing glue and blowing dudes.

CL: Gold paint. Ha, ha!

I: Gold paint?

CL: It's got methylphosphonate—that's why the kids like the gold—gets you higher than any other color.

SM: How the hell do you know that?

CL: I sprayed finish for four years. Three years?

SM: Did you always go like mask off when you were spraying that shit?

CL: No. That's like some Mexican-kid-from-the-70s shit. I used to know a lot of tweakers. But paint just makes you nauseous. That's why I always wore my respirator. You getting this?

I: Yeah.

CL: Anyway, I'd rather shrink my frontal lobe with some quality bourbon.

I: Zoning regulations factor heavily into your political consciousness. True or false?

CL: God, my back.

SM: Off to the point? Twenty-five minutes round trip.

CL: Hey, I can't stand up. Somebody give me a hand.

88.

It was Thursday night, which meant karaoke, free dance lessons, and half-price well drinks at Little Rock's bikini rodeo show warehouse. The parking lot was packed. College bros threw cigarette butts out their truck windows at each other's faces as they fought over the best parking spots. Then they got out of their trucks, rolled up their sleeves, and brawled.

The bikini girls were all lined up and ready to go. The announcer was drinking rye whiskey from the bottle, also ready to go. The bull, which was mechanical, was newly greased and as ready as it would ever be. The college bros came pouring in.

"First up, in the red top and the hot jean cutoffs, a spicy little thing from Pine Bluff, it's Suuuzzz-aaannne!"

She took one last swig of Fireball. Tightened her ponytail. Wiggled her ass up to the monstrous machine. Hopped on and held tight to the leather straps.

"Wooh!"

"Yeah, yeah!"

"Get it, girl!"

The dudes cheered and the bull began to buck. Slowly at first, making the girl rock up and down like riding a bike over giant bubbles. Then she swayed side to side, making her hair fly like a summer breeze over a wheat field. Then the bull became erratic, showing its power and violence. The bros focused in on the girl's breasts and waited for things to get interesting.

Over by the bar, curled up on a seedy-looking couch, Sweet Jesus opened his eyes. Groaning, he sat up, looked around. The lamp by his head cast a mellow light. A cloud of dust and a few gnats circled the glowing bulb. Otherwise, the warehouse was dark and still. Clint and Richie were quietly working out an angle for a trick shot on the pool table. A few other bathrobed guys were passed out on their bar stools.

Sweet Jesus—Mike—rubbed his temples, yawned, and

stretched. For the first time in what seemed like several life-times, he felt amazing, rejuvenated to the fullest. His mind was clear, totally wiped clean of all memories, even imagined memories, like visions of bikini girls riding mechanical bulls. No, he remembered one thing: his puke bucket. Looking over the edge of the couch, he was relieved to see that the bucket had been taken away.

It was happening. Suzanne's top was coming undone. The bros were losing their shit, yelling like wolves and spilling beer all over themselves. Suzanne panicked. She liked her breasts well enough, but she didn't like the idea of them flopping around every which way like epileptic twins just learning to dance. But it wasn't too late yet. She reached one hand up to her chest to catch the strap that was about to come loose. At that same moment, the mechanical monster lunged forward, simultaneously bucking counter-clockwise...

"Aaaannnnddd," said the announcer, "DOWN she goes!"

89.

This is the womb, thought Robbie Cox. I am not dead. Al-though it would appear as though I have died, I have not. I am being reborn.

The rebirthing process, of course, is the ultimate test of po-litical acumen. Step one of the test is to acquaint oneself with the nature of the womb. One must consider one's womb care-fully. Is it:

A) A representation of the world that is yet to come?

B) The antithesis of all that one holds dear in terms of one's political aspirations?

C) A non-thing to the extent that its relation to outside

things does not exist?

Robbie Cox walked in circles for days, weeks, quite possibly for years or centuries. Could the rebirthing process go on forever? Was this the womb of no return?

Step two of the test is to not succumb to one's sense of never getting out of here alive, but instead to hold strong to the knowledge that it's all worth the inconvenience for the sake of one's political acumen.

Step three of the test is to avoid all snake pits, for it would be incomprehensible for a place like this (see step one on acquainting oneself with one's womb) to not have a pit of snakes.

Step four of the test is to trounce a minotaur—or some other mythological creature (but preferably a minotaur).

Step five of the test is to not abandon one's broader mission, which existed before and will doubtlessly carry on after one's time spent in this most abysmally hellish of wombs.

90.

Hi-ya kids! Here we are at the Superhero Fashion Show! Come on, let's check it out!

This year, it's all about the private eye look: the dark trench coat, the black tie, the custom-fit fedora. Here's Russian diplomat Vlad Budnikov coming down the runway. Wow! Look at that trench coat flutter! At a glance you'd mistake it for last year's hit, the five-meter cape!

Now here's something different. Looks like somebody's going all in for the hobo couture style. I do like the snug beany, the tattered army jacket... But those boots? My god, no! But he's getting the votes with that strut—mmm, hmm! Listen to that crowd!

But now it's time for a sneak peak at what's to come! Superheroes in Swimsuits! Take a look at Australian heartthrob Cricket Backwater taking a dip in the pool with India's latest addition to the political elite...Manali Kiri!

Talk about a superhero bikini bod! One look at her and crime just stops! Saving the world—with Manali Kiri—it's all in the hips!

And now a message from Political Tees, your one-stop shop for all the latest political slogan hats, panties, t-shirts, and more! Even socks!

91.

Killian stared out his bedroom window. Blinking, his eyes were so glazed with boredom you'd think he was tasked with watching molasses drip. It was mid-afternoon. He hadn't left his house for two days. He was trying to figure things out. Which meant waiting to get tired enough to get back to sleep. All the answers seemed to be in his dreams.

Daydreams didn't cut it. They were just lame. Like this one now of Uncle Jon walking down the sidewalk. Keeping his head down and shoulders slouched. Looking like an oversized sewer rat coming out of the blue. Scurrying along, apparently headed to Killian's house.

There was a knock at the door. Killian gave a start. Daydream Uncle Jon wasn't so much of a daydream after all.

The knock came again.

"I'm coming!" Killian's mom screamed. His dad would have screamed, too, if he hadn't died some time ago. The plague took him and his miserable scream along with the first large-scale batch of townsfolk.

Killian froze and listened just long enough. Uncle Jon for sure wasn't coming over just to say hello. His tone was authoritative and demanding—things it rarely had been pre-plague.

Quietly, Killian opened his bedroom window. It was a long way down. But he told himself. Don't worry. I've done this before in my dreams, I think.

Why do this? He didn't have time to wonder. But he had to. It was something about his instincts, which he was beginning to feel were superhero instincts, like a natural aversion to anything having to do with the world ending. His instincts now were telling him to go.

He had one leg out the window and was about to swing the other out when he saw—

92.

A group of bearded guys in bathrobes stood on the street, looking up at Killian's bedroom. They were holding up signs apparently directed at nothing in particular—except for Killian with his leg dangling out the window.

Their signs read: LIBERATE DUDEBUDDY.

You've never seen such expressionless faces in your life as they had. Their faces were so expressionless, it was like they were the saints of expressionless faces. Possibly they were a little bored-looking, too—but with intensity about it. Bored, expressionless intensity.

In the back of the group, Sweet Jesus held his sign stiff as an extra limb cast in iron. He didn't look up at Killian. He just focused his attention on the back of the guy's head in front of him. It took all his effort not to lose the expressionless face he held. His fake beard was begging to be adjusted and scratched.

"What's the matter, Mike?" said Clint, the bearded guy beside Sweet Jesus. "You look a little disconcerted."

"Huh?" Sweet Jesus answered, smiling vaguely, letting his eyes wander loosely in his head.

He glanced up at Killian just then. He couldn't help it. He saw Killian slip his second leg out over the edge of his window.

93.

Killian was out of sight by now. He'd jumped down from his bedroom and run empty handed away from town, for the forest. If he was hoping to get away and never be seen again, it was a good tactic. The forest didn't lead anywhere, just to the foothills of a mountain range. Beyond that, eventually there was a desert.

Sweet Jesus, Clint, and the other guys in bathrobes hung around outside Killian's house for a while. They leaned against their LIBERATE DUDEBUDDY signs and passed around a bottle of whiskey.

"Where to next?" asked Clint.

"There's gotta be a bar in this town," said Richie.

"For all the good it'll do," said Clint, pulling his beard down under his chin, "if all the bartenders are dead."

From inside the house, there came a hair-raising shriek. It was a woman's shriek, the kind where you might assume that there was a new death metal band in town.

"Damn," said Clint.

"Wow," said Richie.

They looked at each other and then at the house, which had again fallen silent. Clint was the first to move. The rest of the guys followed with Sweet Jesus taking up the rear.

They made it up to the porch and stood there like a little mob of churchgoing propagandists. Clint pressed his ear against the door and listened while Richie tried to peak through a window. With a shrug, Clint opened the door and walked inside. The others followed on tiptoes, arranging their beards and the belts on their bathrobes as if to make themselves presentable.

"Dr. Gilbert?" called Clint, referring to Uncle Jon by his professional name.

No response.

Clint shrugged again and started moving up the stairs.

At the front door, hesitating only for a moment, Sweet Jesus slowly backed away. Once outside, he turned and shuffled down the front steps. He was running away at top speed when there came another terrifying shriek from the house. As he bolted across the street and headed for the forest in the distance, the shriek quickly faded into the gloomy stillness of the afternoon.

94.

What is this place, a comic book club for schizophrenics? HAH! Nope, but good guess!

Comic book clippings were everywhere. Taped on the walls, taped to the ceiling, scattered on tables, piling up on the floor. There were arrows drawn in black marker, things circled in red, notes scribbled haphazardly in ink.

"Copyeditor's Headquarters" is what we had started calling this place. But it might as well have been a hangout for adolescent, funny papers-obsessed serial killers. Or a comic book club for schizos.

If you were just drunk enough, you could really start to see the pieces connecting. But all drunkenness aside, there was something concrete to be said about Alalia, Secretary of Interstellar Space Stations.

Here's what we knew.

Alalia was a character back in the days when comic books were openly misogynistic, so go figure that she was a secretary. Also she was healthily endowed. I mean that in terms of her side-view especially. When she turned to the side, there was plenty of womanly figure to run your eyes over. You know that's what they had in mind when they drew her, those misogynistic pricks.

We didn't pay much attention to Alalia at first. But then Emma—a tour-de-force of a copyeditor, but also one shy cookie—admitted that she'd been holding out on us. And that's when she brought out a few copies of an especially racy series of comic books. Flipping through them, it was quite the porno show.

Alalia was a star character in the series. At one point, between raucous affairs with international warlords and such, she received a summons from a mysterious individual in Dudebuddy Nation. The details are scarce, but the mysterious individual turned out to be a rather high-up character in the DLF (Dudebuddy Liberation Front).

His name was Meriwether.

Meriwether knew all about Alalia. He knew, for example, that she was brought up in the forbidden religion—that she was a believer in the Dudebuddy.

Then they fell in love. Or at least Alalia fell in love. Meriwether had a complicated relationship with love. Turned out he came from another dimension, one where love isn't so high up on the list of things to feel. That's sort of implied, at least. With comic books, character development can be a bit wishy-washy. As opposed to the love scenes. The love scenes were as palpable and detailed as if you were there watching.

As the wild sex scenes carried on, details cropped up about Meriwether's racket. Meriwether was liaison to the Dude-buddy, who in turn was the ruler by default of the dimension Meriwether came from. (Granted, you'd miss all this if you got wrapped up too much in the nudity and fornication, but if you're paying attention it's all right there in the dialogue bubbles.)

Dudebuddy was the enemy of politics. He couldn't stand politics. All he wanted to do was bring an end to politics. But there was one problem. He was allergic to it. If he got near it, his soul would leak away.

Initially, he'd hoped to rid the universe of politics by spreading the liberating news of his politics-less dimension as a sort of religion. People in the political dimension would wake up from dreams in a religious fervor, their minds flooded with images of Dudebuddy chilling out on a tropical island, beckoning with endless cheer to join him in this picture of ultimate good times, glamour, and sexually-charged bliss.

After a few nights of these dreams, those who were open to them would experience an added detail: Dudebuddy, your new best friend and likely savior, was locked out from entering your world. He wanted to come and meet you and bring you back with him, but he couldn't. The authority figures in your world wouldn't allow it. By the seventh night of dreams, the faithful believers would wake up with the battle cry, "Liberate

Dudebuddy."

"Liberate Dudebuddy?" Emma asked. She pretended like she didn't know. We reminded her of the ancient document from back at the office. How it was a flyer with the same message—and it predated the comic book by at least a few thousand years.

"Yeah but, what does it mean?"

Here's a thought, we all burst out. (We were pinning notes and things like crazy to the garage walls. Drawing lines between comic clippings, guzzling beer.) It's evidence that Dudebuddy Nation isn't just a comic book, but a real place in its own dimension. Or maybe it's just a missing page from a really old comic book, someone suggested, who was drunk. Maybe, others of us shouted. Who knows?!

95.

We all said goodbye to each other, you know, around dinner time. There comes a point (and it usually coincides with getting hungry) when the problems of the world just kind of— It's just hard to care anymore. That's what I mean. You've got to suspend your belief in all things going to hell. Otherwise, how could you eat if the world is going to end at any moment? And you've got to eat!

I went home with Emma. She invited me over to her place for crepes with avocados and sun dried tomatoes. She lived in an apartment nearby. I may have been there a time or two. Once when she was out of town and her goldfish needed someone to feed it. Another time for a copyeditor's book club. I hadn't read the book to be discussed and it turned out that no one else had, either. Except for Emma. So she just gave us a brief summary and then we all went home, pretending not to be embarrassed for ourselves.

"How's Catwoman?" I asked when we got to her place, referring to her goldfish.

"I don't know," said Emma. "Look." She pointed. I went over and peered into the tank.

"She's a little off color?" I said, kind of as a question, trying to be polite about it.

"I know. You think it's a disease?"

"Do goldfishes get diseases?"

This was like all my conversations lately. Full of weird questions, usually about death. No one really knows what they're talking about when they're talking about death.

Then we made crepes and ate politely. Didn't have much to say at that point. Didn't even bring up ancient documents or the things that we'd pieced together from the comic books. Catwoman was looking pretty bad. Getting worse by the minute. She was turning black with more and more dark splotches. We finished our crepes like nothing was the matter.

I was relieved when the meal was over. I already had a good excuse lined up to leave early. It was another long day ahead. First to the office bright and early, then to the garage.

"Don't go," said Emma, shyly. "Can't you stay?"

"I could, but... You mean stay the night?"

"I just mean... What if Catwoman dies?"

"Do you think she will?"

We looked over at the fish bowl. Couldn't quite tell if Catwoman was swimming or floating.

After a moment, Emma shrugged. "It's just a goldfish," she said.

96.

You can spend a lot of time in a forest and still think that it's nothing but a bunch of dumb trees. But forests don't need your opinion. Unlike cities—which are nothing but a bunch of buildings that probably can't wait to crumble to the ground—forests take care of themselves.

The moment he entered the forest, Sweet Jesus felt right at home. He threw off his bathrobe and ran free and wild like a—

He stopped. Wait a moment, he thought, collecting himself. Well, that was rather impulsive of me! Laughing off his exuberance, he went back a few steps to retrieve his robe. What if it gets cold and I'm stuck out here naked? he thought, sober minded. So, he kept the robe. But now he wore it tied around his waist like a kilt.

At this point, he couldn't even remember where the rest of his clothes had gone. Likely they were back at the warehouse in Arkansas. A world away, a lifetime ago, it seemed. Nearly as long ago as the days at Homunculus Castle.

What's worse, he wondered, Homunculus Castle or the Arkansas warehouse? They were both places he felt he could never return to. Coincidentally, they both represented opposite forces in the fight to bring about the world's end.

Sweet Jesus didn't know what it all meant. But he knew he didn't like holding sacrilegious protest signs and being called Mike. Also, he knew all along he wasn't one to be brainwashed that easily.

97.

For one whole day, the world lost its shit over the disappearance of Robbie Cox. On that day, the official POLITICAL OP-ED piece went something like this:

Robbie Cox? Sure, I'll admit it: at this point, he's probably screwed. My best guess is, he cheated on his taxes (who hasn't?!) and that finally caught up with him in a bad way, so now he's changed his name and is walking among us in homeless garb till the whole thing's blown over (when the world ends, you might say, if you want to get fatalistic about it—hah!). Either that or he's hanging out with Militant King X talking shop and wondering what to do with himself when the political paparazzi finally catch on.

In other news that day, common people were all up in arms, passing around a petition, demanding things like:

The return of Robbie Cox to his regular "Let's Save the World Together Guys" programing.

A justification for the anxiety-provoking loss of high quality entertainment formerly available through Robbie's presence in the public spotlight.

An apology for Erectalphlegm Syndrome, not only as a lame threat to human existence, but also as a thing that Robbie Cox, of all people, has been responsible for following up on.

Or, to paraphrase a section of the most widely circulated petition:

We expect more from the people who give us the political cartoons which we watch all the time. Specifically, we don't want to sit back and watch the world end unless we've got Robbie Cox on the front lines of the superheroes, so that we can watch him save it. Even more specifically, we demand the return of Cox starting tonight to his regular scheduled programing of not only the evening news but also his weekly feature on the sitcom "Let's Save the World Together Guys."

This petition got about ten million signatures in one day—the day the shit hit the fan re. Robbie Cox's disappearance. The petition was just the beginning. Riots on the streets were planned, sit ins, walk outs, and any other form of protest people could think of.

Then time passed. About a day or two. At that point, the universal outrage just sort of lost its steam. The average person more or less forgot all about Robbie Cox. Another day or two went by and the regular scheduled programming simply continued on without him—and no one seemed to know the difference.

98.

Killian was lying under a tree on a bed of pine needles and dirt, curled up on his side, eyes forced shut, hands pressing against his ears like trying to squeeze a watermelon till it burst. He looked about as tranquil as the start of a boxing match.

The sun was on its way down—it would set within the next hour or two. But it was still light enough to safely say that ghosts wouldn't be out quite yet. Only, there was a ghost. Right out in the open, not even hiding behind a tree. Although moving slowly and with a certain poise, it was real enough to step on bugs and break sticks every few paces. Even Killian in his balled-up, ears-muffled state could sense it approaching.

One of Killian's eyes edged open. Was he just paranoid? He moved his hands to listen. Then he sat bolt upright when the ghost blurted out: "Hey kid, you alright?"

"I'm sleeping," said Killing irritably, easing back down onto the ground. He recognized the "ghost" as one of the bathrobed guys.

"With your hands on your ears like that?" asked the guy, tightening the bathrobe around his waist.

"The birds are chirping."

"I don't hear any birds."

"Well, they were!"

Killian resumed his sleeping position: curled up, eyes pressed closed, hands on his ears.

"Hey..." said the guy, tapping Killian on the shoulder. "Hey... Hello? You recognize me, don't you?"

"You're Sweet Jesus," said Killian, stubbornly locked into his sleeping position, "but who cares. You're the same as everyone else. I'm not surprised one bit you got that white robe on."

"I'd take it off, but I'd be naked."

"I'm trying to sleep."

"Are you tired? You don't seem very—"

"If I sleep, I can stop what's happening." He glared at Sweet Jesus accusingly, as if to say, "I can stop you."

"I'd like to know what you mean."

When Killian answered with silence, Sweet Jesus stated:

"I could be wrong, but I believe we're on the same side. I hope that is true, because then we could help each other. So, if you'll allow me the honor..."

Still Killian said nothing. But his glare softened.

"I don't know exactly what's happening," Sweet Jesus confided, taking a seat on the ground next to Killian, "but I have a fair idea. The guys in the bathrobes came to your house because they were following your uncle, Dr. Gilbert. They were keeping an eye on him to make sure he followed through with his next step. Apparently the giant virus he discovered and proliferated is the only real threat to the world. Erectalphlegm Syndrome, global nuclear war, the rogue black hole, and all the rest of the ten threats are just theoretical backup plans. The Dudebuddy Liberation Front is counting on your uncle's virus to spread. But to ensure that it does, they need his ongoing cooperation."

"Why do they want the world to end so bad?"

"It's the only way they know to wipe out politics. It's in the lifeblood of our species. We're hard wired for it. If they want to get rid of politics, they have to get rid of us. Although, apparently they do want to keep some of us around."

"If they want to kill us so bad, why don't they just do it themselves?"

"You mean instead of using your uncle?"

"Yeah!"

"They can't; that's my guess. To do so would be a political act. And they're totally against political acts. According to legend, they use liaisons to accomplish any act that could be considered politics. That's why they're keeping some of us politicians alive, to serve as their liaisons. It's all orchestrated by a guy named Meriwether, who apparently is some kind of interstellar pirate for him."

"So, they're the bad guys, right?"

"I'd say so."

"What happens if they win?"

"If they win? For one thing, that would mean the world would be destroyed. But, also, once the universe is freed from politics, then Dudebuddy could expand his chilled-out, politics-free lifestyle way behind his current dimension. I imagine he's probably cramped up in some shallow dimension that, compared to ours, is like a tiny island in the middle of the ocean. I imagine he's bored."

Killian thought for a moment. He made a mental note, clarifying his mission: must defeat Dudebuddy. It was an uneasy thought to swallow. All his life, starting with his early childhood dreams, he'd believed that Dudebuddy was like God— beyond politics, but in a neutral, peaceful way. That belief was the best part about life. If you believe in someone as powerful as that, then you don't have to spend every moment scared of your parents and uncertain of things to come. You can feel empowered no matter what.

But then you find out that this same guy is the reason your one true love got killed. Then you have a whole different view of things. Maybe if only Jenny were still alive. Maybe then Killian wouldn't suddenly feel like he had lost his religion.

"Okay, now can I try to sleep?" he asked.

99.

Interview with a Caucasian landowner, pt. 7: "At the Courthouse" (WARNING: This interview series is unedited. Anytime you feel aggrieved, take comfort in knowing there are lots of terrible people in the world. If you want to know your chances of whether or not you're one of them, here's a coin to flip.)

INTERVIEWER: Is this the first time someone has ever tried to sue your ass off, or is this a regular occurrence?

CAUCASIAN LANDOWNER: Being sued, in this country, is a right of passage. I'm proud to be sued! Do you see this tie? This is the tie of a fighter! Anyone else around here want to file claims? Huh?

I: I've never seen you quite so agitated.

CL: Gold paint!

I: Come again?

CL: You heard me!

I: I see.

CL: Yeah, feelin' good! It's just the nausea that's a bitch.

I: True or false: bribing a judge is morally repugnant. And you'd never do it.

CL: Never? Hah! I'd try anything for the right price.

I: How much would you have to be paid to bribe a judge?

CL: Shit, I'd do that just for the hell of it. So long as I got my money back. I mean the money I'd have to spend to bribe the guy. Unless you're talking in terms of sexual favors.

I: Worst case scenario, what, all told, is it you stand to lose today?

CL: Five million! Ha, ha! As if I— HA, HA, HA!

I: For her injuries and her emotional distress?

CL: Yeah, it's just a lot of legal BS.

I: But you're not worried? I understand the girl—what's her name?—the bikini girl has quite the shark for a lawyer.

CL: I'll kick him in the nuts! Do you see this tie?

I: The big question is, will you ever boat again?

CL: That's her boyfriend right there. With the possum's ass for a face. Bet he can't stand the fact that I've got a boat. That I had his girl on my boat. That I have a fucking picket fence and when I go to a steakhouse, I order whatever the hell I want.

I: When the world ends, would you rather be the first to die, or the last?

CL: She's never allowed on it ever again. That's one thing for sure. Every bitch from now on signs a liability waiver or she can find her own damn boat.

I: Kind of puts everything in perspective, the idea of five million. Just like that.

CL: Hah!

100.

Complete darkness isn't so bad after a while. It has its own sort of charm. Like the way it gives the impression of being endless and eternal. Sure, maybe you're stuck underground in a snake-pit-ridden cave, but with such profound darkness, it's almost like you can look out and stare into eternity in all directions, all the time.

Robbie Cox spent most of his waking hours frying up snakes. He didn't like the idea of a snake pit until he found one. Then he found another one. And then a third. It turned out that a whole section of the caves was almost nothing but snake pits. Once he got used to them, he never wanted to leave.

If there's one goal that makes life worth living, it's to have a fear and to conquer it. Then, once you've conquered it to your liking, it's best to exploit the bounty of your conquest. That's good living.

Robbie didn't have fire, but if he closed his eyes hard enough, he would eventually see something that looked like fire. After catching a snake, he'd squeeze his eyes tight while wringing the snake with one hand on its head and the other on its tale. In his mind, the effect was just like roasting a pig on a spit. He'd roast the snake until his eyes began to tear up. Then he'd sample a few scales, pinching them off delicately with his front teeth. If they were too tough and chewy, he'd keep wringing. Eventually, he'd have a well-wrung snake. If you were to ask, he'd tell you that's about the same as a bloody-rare steak.

One day, Robbie was wringing out his third snake for breakfast when suddenly he froze. He heard something. In the darkness, his senses were honed to the point of preternatural accuracy. It wasn't so much that he heard a sound, but that he felt it.

"Who's there?" he asked. The power in his voice was a terrible shock. It had been so long since he had spoken, he had forgotten the power of his own voice. So that's what it sounds like to be a champion politician, he thought.

"Shh! Act natural!" came the immediate response, whispered in a heavy Arabic accent.

"What? Hey, who's—"

"Do not stob! Keeb wringing ze snake!"

Confused, Robbie returned to his breakfast-making. The snake was nearly well-wrung, but he kept wringing, more vigorously than ever.

"You cannot see me," said the voice, "but I can see you. Also, George can see you. She has blaced cameras all about zese cabes."

"Who are you?" Robbie asked. The voice was undeniably distinct, yet he couldn't quite place it.

"Keeb wringing. Do not stob!"

"Wait…" Robbie gave the snake a nibble at its midsection. "I think it's done."

"Okay. Whatever you must do. Just do not look in my direction. We cannot let zat woman George know it's me here."

It struck Robbie that there was only one person he could be speaking to. Yet it didn't make sense.

"Why should I listen to you?" he asked, ripping the head off the snake with one swift yank. "And give me one good reason why I shouldn't throw you to the snakes."

"Calm you self! You want boz us dead? Your George double cross you from ze start. And now she double cross me! Ze King X! She but you here to sit on you. To keep you alive for her marketing blan. She use me for ze same blan. Crazy woman! She no joke wants to see ze world destroyed! Haha, haha!"

"So that's the ultimate scenario right there, huh? Well, that's easy enough. Just let me out of here, and I'll make sure 'ze crazy woman George' can't double cross anyone ever again. How about that?"

"Oh, dumb, dumb bolitician. Zat's you! So dumb!"

"Okay, how about this, then. I'll just throw you to the snakes. Fatten them up so I have something better to chew on. Then I'll eventually die down here. And George wins. And the snakes win. That sound better to you?"

"Keeb eating! You talk too much and George she have suspicion. Listen, Cox, I halb you outa here. But to do it, we must fake your dez. You must fling you-self to ze snakes."

"Right," said Robbie, munching on raw snake belly, "throw me to the snakes. Sure, that sounds like a great plan."

101.

"I'm convinced, now more than ever. Working is for the feudal classes, not me."

In their cramped apartment, Al leaned against the door-frame of the bathroom. He sipped a glass of water while his buddy Charlie vomited into the toilet. After watching for a moment, Al turned away with a repulsed look on his face.

He set the glass of water on the bedside table, then slumped down heavily on the bed next to Trista. She was sixteen. Al was over six-hundred.

"Me too," said Trista, fingering a little bag of heroin. "Work can suck it."

Al waited for a moment to speak, until Charlie had finished up puking. Then he didn't know what to say. He was staring at Trista, mesmerized by the obsessive care she took in fiddling with the little dose of white powder.

"He'll be like that for another week or two," she said, casually explaining what to expect when kicking heroin cold turkey. Al liked her voice. It was calming but ferocious, like she was holding a grudge for something that could easily be fixed, but it was simply more fun to keep it broken.

"We'll see," said Al. "He's tough."

She shook her head. "It doesn't matter. A habit like he had wipes out all your endorphins and shit. It's like when you move your eyes"—she tilted her head theatrically and moved her eyes from one side to the other—"even just doing that causes some amount of pain. But you don't notice it because your endorphins block the pain. It's like that for every part of your body. Your toes and your guts and all. When you can't get a fix, you feel every microscopic form of agony in places you didn't even know existed. And also there's the sweating and the nausea."

Al waited for the sound of Charlie's puking to start up again. About a second passed and—

"BREA-EEE-AWWWK"

Al laughed, "Heh."

"Okay," Trista blurted out, her tone completely changed. She set down the heroin and turned to face Al directly for the first time. "What is the deal with monarchy. God! Like, isn't it proved just a lame form of politics?"

"It's not—AH, EH—you don't—WRAAW," Charlie yelled from the bathroom, choking on his vomit, and then vomiting.

"He's right," said Al, patiently. "There's quite a bit of misinformation about monarchies out there. To me, it's obviously the preferred way of having a superhero governance. When ruled by a monarch, there is greater unity in a nation."

"SOVEREIGNTY FOREVER—BLEHHH!"

"Yes, indeed," said Al. "A king or a queen is more often than not highly respected by the people, which brings a nation together. In addition, monarchs are uniquely suited to rule a nation in that they are educated and trained for the position from a very young age. More than any other type of superhero, they understand and value their role as national figurehead."

"AND POLICIES OF— OF—"

"Of course... As I was just about to say—"

"OF— WREHHH!"

"When there is only one person in charge of decision-making, decisions are arrived at quickly, painlessly. Achieving a new policy to improve the lives of the people is as simple as, for example, waiving one's hand—or scepter."

"How do you know what's best?" Trista yelled, delicately holding her drug equipment. "And what if I want to play superhero next, huh? What, I can't do it just because I wasn't born into it? That is just so...so...! It's just lame! What if I'm the best superhero there is, no matter who my parents are? And you mean that just doesn't matter because in your system, you're the superhero no matter what? I mean... God!"

Charlie staggered out of the bathroom just then. He made a great effort to pull himself together. He was shaking, drooling, and visibly sweating through ever last pore, but at least he was standing on his own two legs and, for once, not spewing his guts out.

"I give up," he said, forcing a tragic smile. "I can't go on. Just one shot. Just one little taste."

Al wasn't sure what might happen next. All that he could think was, "I'm not going back to work. Never again. Especially not to support this pathetic habit!" He looked at Trista, startled to hear her let out a laugh.

"Sorry, pal," said Trista, coming to her feet. She walked over to him, shaking her head with a mother's sympathy. "I promise we won't mention politics anymore, okay? I know how you don't like taking any kind of criticism. How you'd rather just live in your little fantasy world." She put an arm around his broad, lumpy shoulder. "Here, I'll help you back to the toilet."

102.

Several days passed before Eleanor George noticed that Robbie Cox had vanished from her monitors. When she finally happened to realize that he was nowhere to be seen, she called Militant King X. No luck. After several unanswered calls, she called his second in command. Still, no answer.

"Becky," she said into her intercom, "cancel my next meeting."

"Should I reschedule it for—"

"Yes, that would be fine."

George poured herself a glass of gin and sat down before her computer, slightly trembling. "Goddamn you, Robbie," she said, watching the monitors closely as she ran the recordings in reverse.

She went back in time five minutes...an hour...ten hours... twenty hours... She was deep into the second day in reverse when she paused to take a long drink. Again she called Militant King X. And again, no answer. She cleared her throat nervously. "What a bloody mess," she said, now going back in time forty hours. Three days. How had she not checked the monitors for three days? Three and half days! Four days! Four and a—

Wait. There he was. He was there on the fourth day. Standing beside a snake pit, tearing off the head of one of those horrible snakes. "Now I remember why I stopped watching," George thought to herself, getting up to pour herself more gin. She was only half inclined to watch what might happen next. She thought about calling Becky, her secretary, into her office to continue the investigation. But then again, there would be too much to explain. Out of context, it would seem dubious, to say the least. And of course there was no way to add context. It was too absurd. Along with the rest of the world, Becky thought Robbie Cox was dead.

So, she settled into watching, going forward from the point right before he disappeared. The scene was anything but unusual. At least, it wasn't like he was doing anything blatantly suspicious. He was simply ripping the head off an underground serpent, just as he had been doing for the past several weeks.

But if he wasn't attempting an escape, what could possibly have happened to make him suddenly disappear?

George was tempted to skip ahead to the moment of his disappearance. But she stopped herself from doing so. Perhaps there were clues she could pick up that might become important.

He was talking to himself, she noted. He stopped wringing the snake for a moment and actually appeared to be engaging in a dialogue. Perhaps he wasn't simply talking to himself? But then he was at it again: wringing the snake more viciously than ever. Then he tore off the snake's head. For the first time, George didn't look away as he bit into the body of the scaly creature. Something about the way he chewed kept her attention. It was like he was talking between mouthfuls. It was the most disgusting show of bad manners she had ever seen.

She stiffened, her eyes narrowed. It seemed undeniable that he was talking to someone. The way he projected his speech while chewing on snake guts—it wasn't the way a madman talks to himself. Take away the snake meat, and it was the way a normal person converses.

Her suspicions growing, she watched as Robbie Cox walked down the corridor of snake pits. Still holding half a snake, he periodically whipped the carcass around below his heels, beating away the snakes that came at him with jaws snapping. He seemed to be studying the snake pits. Twice he turned, yelled something, gestured toward a pit. (Who was he talking to?) Finally he stopped and knelt on one knee beside a relatively small hole in the ground. It was only a few feet across. Studying the hole, Robbie suddenly lashed out with the snake carcass, swatting away a quick-moving serpent right as it leapt for his ass. Then he stood up. He tossed the snake carcass aside, stretched his arms up to the ceiling of the cave, and hopped right down into the open mouth of the snake pit.

For several minutes, Eleanor George continue to watch the screen. She hardly blinked. Nothing happened. Even the snakes seemed to have ceased to slither. It was like time had stopped.

Slowly, she pushed back her chair and came to her feet. With a hand resting for support on the desk, she took down the rest of her gin. She found herself dialing the number once again for Militant King X. The call rang and rang. On the screen, a group of snakes had now started a battle amongst themselves. She could almost hear them hiss, hear the sound of their fangs sinking into each other's scaly flesh. Just then the call answered. Like one of the snakes hissing hello, Militant King X's voice came through the line.

103.

Down in the subconscious place where dreams happen, there's a world where everything takes place just like in cartoon shows. It's all LOUD COLORS and BRIGHT LIGHTS and SUPERHEROES and HOT SEX, even when you're just looking for the gardening channel.

Killian slipped from one world of dreams to another, opening a door, closing it, climbing up a level, peeking through a series of windows, diving into a whirlpool of half-conceived dreamlands, slipping into one at random, running down a long hall, busting through a screen, finding himself on a stage, taking a seat in the back, leaning too far back and ending up in space.

He floated for a time. In the silence, a force of some kind pulled at him in the darkness. Stuck in a peculiar posture, like a paper cutout waiting to be placed into a collage, he felt his body being sucked into some unseen vortex. The time for making choices had come and gone. Now it was up to the vortex to decide. The speed of things was like what must go through a surfer's head before going down in a bone-crushing wipeout. Terribly fast, but the longest moment of his life.

Killian wasn't surprised when he found himself in the world of LOUD COLORS. He usually entered it screaming like that. Also, in dreams, there isn't such a thing as a surprise. Everything simply comes at you as it is. And just like that, suddenly you're the star of our own cartoon show.

Jenny was sitting on a park bench reading a magazine. Her legs were crossed, her hair was down. She let the magazine slowly drop to her knee. Something about this movement told Killian that she had been expecting him. He took the seat beside her on the bench while she gazed off in the opposite direction. He couldn't see her face. Even when she turned to address him, still he couldn't make out her features, as if her eyes, nose, and mouth were hiding someplace far off in the distance where her gaze had been fixed.

"You were supposed to save me," she said. "You were supposed to save me. You were supposed to save me." She went back to reading her magazine.

"Everything went wrong," said Killian. "It wasn't supposed to happen like that."

The bench began to float away. Jenny was now staring off into a great distance straight ahead, whether past or future.

"I've never even been kissed before," she sighed. Killian lost his breath and couldn't speak. His heart was racing. "I've never even held hands."

"Me neither."

"You could have. I would have let you."

"What about now?"

"No. After."

"After?"

The bench had sailed out of the park. His legs dangling high up in the air, Killian looked down at a whole city below, where the park was just a small, green square. Outside the city he could see farmland for miles and miles; beyond that, a range of mountains stretched across the full horizon.

"Yes," said Jenny. She was slipping quietly off the bench, her head nodding as though she were falling asleep. "First, you have to find. You have to find. You have to find..."

"Who?" Killian asked, trying desperately to lean forward, to grab her; but he was frozen in place.

The bench began to twirl around and around as the blue sky gave way to darkness. A fierce, mystical wind blew against Killian, putting an incredible weight upon his body and making tears streak across his face. As Jenny slipped from the bench and fell away, her words were caught up in the wind and echoed into the dark vortex that Killian was flailing toward.

"Meriwether. Meriwether. Meriwether."

104.

They were in a motel just outside Memphis with cockroaches in the bathroom and a light shining in from the parking lot like a police investigation. Killian woke up around 4 a.m. He lay there frozen, having completely no idea where in the world he might be. As his eyes drifted shut, he went back over the most vivid moments from his dream. Only when he heard a loud snore nearby from Sweet Jesus did he accept that the dream was truly over. And he was in Memphis, Tennessee. And he'd spent the past two days hitchhiking with this washed up superhero, who turned out to be a champion snorer. And for some reason they were on their way to Little Rock, Arkansas.

"You were supposed to save me. You were supposed to save me. You were supposed to save me," a voice in the back of his mind said, as if his dream was set on manual replay.

It wasn't the sort of dream he'd expected. It was worse. Much worse. He was left feeling sick to his stomach. He had failed to save Jenny. How could he possibly think that he could be of any use in saving the world? When Eleanor George and all the superheroes—led by the DLF—were in on a scheme to see the world's destruction, how could he possibly hope to do anything about that?

Rolling out of bed, he pulled at his twisted shorts and walked unsteadily to the bathroom to pee. Standing on cold tile, blinking in the glare of the bathroom light, he focused on the cockroach crouching by the shower. The bug was staring right at him, its little feelers quivering.

"Meriwether?" said Killian. Pulling his shorts up, he bent down in front of the bug. "Meriwether?" he said again.

His heart raced for a few moments as he watched the bug jigger its feet, almost as if trying to say something. But then it scurried away in a terrified hurry, apparently having just come to its senses and realized a giant monster was staring it down.

Killian shrugged and flushed the toilet.

105.

INTERNATIONAL NEWS AND POLITICS REPORT: The death rate has doubled again. That's the third doubling in two weeks, but the superheroes continue to delay taking action. Political commentators speculate that a strike may be taking place among the superhero ranks. Or there may simply be a failure in leadership. Etc. Etc. Etc.

Note: *Hey, so, this is the copyeditors of your favorite international news and politics publication. We just want to throw in our two cents that if there's anybody out there reading this with even an ounce of authority in terms of shaking up major world events, then you may want to direct your attention to the DLF. That's the Dudebuddy Liberation Front. Haven't you noticed something strange about them lately? Well, you should have! More to the point, you should freaking do something! Before it's too late! Okay, that's all. Just wanted to, you know, throw that out there.*

106.

In his new lab, surrounded by his new lab assistants and all the lab equipment he could ever ask for, Uncle Jon was leaning over a microscope, staring at a human blood cell infected with his special brand of plague. It was a new batch of the plague formula—tweaked slightly, it had the DLF people with the signs and bathrobes all worked up with high hopes.

(I'm coming! his sister—Killian's mom—screamed. He remembered her voice with a shudder. How had she grown so mean? Just the sound of her shrill tone was unnerving.)

The plagued cell held a number of different mysteries. The extreme potency of this batch of virus. How his particular sample...

(She yanked open the door and gasped at the sight of me. Hah! Guess she didn't expect to see me, of all people.)

About a week had passed, but it was still fresh in his mind. How he rushed right into her house, shutting the door behind himself and shushing his sister. Gesturing frantically. Whispering: I have to see Killian. It's extremely important. Is he here?

Something like that.

She retaliated. Possibly just wanting explanations, so that's forgivable... But I didn't have time. Gestured again to shut her up, ran through the house, to the stairs...to the top of the stairs...to Killian's door...knocked just twice, glancing back as she chasing after me. I let myself in. His room was empty.

"Here are the samples you wanted," said a young man's voice, startling Uncle Jon out of his memories. It was one of the lab assistants; he set down an assortment of tiny vials on the table beside the microscope.

"Just set them— Thank you. That's fine."

"Need any more today?"

"Keep them coming."

"For real?"

"Yes! And more slides!"

"Okay, Dr. Gilbert. You got it!"

Each of these things were horribly infectious. One little taste and you're dead. It was all too easy to picture the open sores, the sweat-drenched scalps, the delirious eyes of the infected.

But Uncle Jon was thinking about Killian.

Listen to me! he said to his sister, grabbing her by the arms and forcing her up against the the wall in Killian's room. I have to find him. Where is he?

Why couldn't he forget this scene? This was his sister. Right then, he remembered growing up. Dinner time with mom and dad. Going to school and getting picked on by his friends because they all wanted to date her. He remembered thinking how she was powerful in a magical sense, the way people can only be when you know them really well, and you know what potential they keep stored up deep inside.

Also she was so pretty back then. Pretty, slim, smart, and even fashionable. Hard to imagine now. Nearly impossible, really!

She'd run away, come back, floundered, and eventually gotten married. She'd become miserable, cold, and hard through the years. Her bad luck and her lazy sack of shit of a husband wore her down. Now her husband was dead from the plague (Uncle Jon glanced at the sparkling vials), but she still had Killian.

He's the antidote! whispered Uncle Jon just as there was a knock at the front door, downstairs. He glanced at Killian's bedroom window and saw that it was wide open. So that's what had— He had climbed out. Escaped!

His blood. It's the only possible cure. Without it—

Dr. Gilbert? called a voice from the bottom of the stairs. Was this really happening? That was a thought that crossed his mind. As he looked at his sister and saw that she would have killed him right there and then if she had the strength. And then one of the terrycloth bathrobe-wearing guys entered. And she screamed like I'd never heard anyone scream before.

The tweaked formula was something else. Uncle Jon couldn't quite comprehend how it had become so potent. Perhaps he was some kind of scientific genius after all? He blinked into his microscope and took a deep breath. It was a damn good virus, alright.

107.

Killian and Sweet Jesus arrived at the bus station in Little Rock, Arkansas around six o'clock in the evening. By six-thirty, they were sitting down to plates of barbecue with large portions of baked beans and cornbread. Killian was used to stale sandwiches and the occasional overcooked egg. This was possibly the best meal he'd ever had in his life.

Oddly, no one around here seemed to be quite so worried about the plague. It was like the general state of world affairs just sailed right on past Little Rock, never leaving so much as a politician's fingerprint. In the back of his mind, Killian wondered if the people around here ever even took the time to vote. But between mouthfuls of barbecue, his mind moved on to something else.

"Are you really in the Superhero Hall of Fame?" he asked.

"Yes. Or, I was. My removal is still pending, last I heard."

"What do you mean?"

"Eleanor George, who was my employer, and who also owns the Superhero Hall of Fame Foundation, has reason to want me out of it."

Killian wiped away some sticky barbecue sauce from his cheek with a napkin. He made a sour face. "I don't like her."

"Ah, so you know about her?" Sweet Jesus sipped coffee distractedly. Ever since they'd arrived in Little Rock, he'd seemed nervous.

"I met her with my uncle. We were in her London office, but then we went to Cancun. She's the one using my uncle to destroy the world."

Sweet Jesus waited for Killian to say more, but he fell silent; his mouth was too full to get into the details at the moment. But Sweet Jesus suddenly showed interest in the conversation.

"Did she ever mention Dudebuddy? Or the Dudebuddy Liberation Front?"

"Don't think so..." said Killian, chewing a few more seconds, then swallowing and wiping his face again. "Maybe, I guess? But my uncle mentioned him all the time. I grew up hearing stories and I thought he was... I don't know. It was like he was my best friend. At least in my dreams, he was. I don't know how to explain it. But I'd get in trouble anytime I ever mentioned it. Except for with Uncle Jon. He had the same dreams I did."

The waitress came over just then to ask if Sweet Jesus wanted more coffee.

"Yes, thank you," he said, not making eye contact. He looked down and smiled grimly, apparently waiting for her to leave before he spoke again. The waitress didn't seem to be in any hurry.

Glancing up at the girl's face, but mostly staring at her chest, Killian thought that he'd never seen a person quite like her before. It wasn't just the way she spoke, which came off as goofy in his opinion. It was something different—subtler than that. He just wasn't sure. Then again, he couldn't think clearly about much of anything as she leaned over, her breasts right in front of him, to pour the coffee.

"Maybe we should talk about this later," said Sweet Jesus when the waitress had left.

"Okay."

"Around here, folks don't usually talk about politics."

"Uh-huh. It's weird…"

"Little Rock is, in fact, the least political place in the world. That's why I had to get out of here, so long ago."

They didn't speak much more throughout the meal. When the waitress brought the check, Killian noticed that Sweet Jesus signed his name as "Mike." He figured it was best not to ask what that was about—at least not while they were in Little Rock.

108.

"Wish I could join ya'll," the cab driver grinned, practically winking as Sweet Jesus paid the fare. "I mean, assuming you can get in," said the driver, now talking to Killian. "A bit young for this kinda night out, ain't ya, son?"

Killian wasn't sure what to say. Hopping out of the cab, he threw a glance at Sweet Jesus.

"He'll be alright," said the elderly superhero.

The cab drove way, leaving Killian and Sweet Jesus standing in the expansive parking lot outside the bikini rodeo warehouse. It was well after dark. Rain was just beginning to fall; heavy drops came down sideways with gusts of wind like someone was tearing pieces out of the sky, and outer space was flooding in through the cracks.

Killian looked up at the sky, then stared straight ahead at the shockingly run-down-looking warehouse. He'd never heard the term "urban decay" before, otherwise that's the exact term he'd have on his mind.

"So…this is some kind of a portal, you think?" he asked, as if he was sure there must be some mistake.

"Yes, this is the place. Although…" Sweet Jesus studied the

sea of trucks filling up the lot. He watched as a rowdy group of bros and meatheads walked up to the warehouse. He scowled at the bright neon sign above the entrance, which was complete with the image of a girl in a hot pink bikini riding a bull—a detail that certainly wasn't there before. "Although, business seems to have picked up quite a bit since I was last here."

"What do you mean?" asked Killian, looking around at a completely vacant lot. Even the wind didn't have so much as a lost newspaper to blow against.

"Before, this lot was deserted, the warehouse abandoned-looking. Now...there's got to be almost a hundred people here."

"Huh? This doesn't look like a hundred people to me!"

"But look at these trucks."

"What trucks?"

Sweet Jesus didn't answer. He had to think. Something didn't seem right. One glance at Killian and he could see that his companion wasn't completely present. With each step toward the entrance, Killian grew further and further away.

"You may be on your own soon."

"I can't hear you...!" Killian shouted, his face showing signs of distress.

"I said you may be on your own soon!"

"What? It's so windy! Why are you so blurry?!"

"I can't join you! I don't know why! But..." Killian had all but vanished. Suddenly Sweet Jesus was shouting at a ghost, or perhaps something more like a memory. "But you'll know what to do!" he shouted, hopelessly.

And then, Killian was gone. Sweet Jesus stood at the entrance of the warehouse. He shook his head, wondering if there was anything he could do to join his young friend. He looked back at the overflowing parking lot, then up at the sky, which was just beginning to rumble with approaching thunder. Feeling the glow of the neon sign on his face, Sweet Jesus swore under his breath and reached for the door handle.

Inside, sure enough, it was just a typical southern bar with bad lighting and gimmicky floorshows. There was no long hallway, and the bouncer didn't offer him a bathrobe. For a moment, he could almost picture Killian standing off to the side and slipping into a white bathrobe that somehow fit him just perfectly. But the image flitted away as quickly as it had come. Checking the time, Sweet Jesus went to order a beer.

109.

When Robbie jumped down into the snake pit, he fell for only a few moments before splashing into a sea of snakes. By the time he lost momentum in his fall, he was buried well over his head. It took a good deal of squirming, but at last he maneuvered himself so that his head was facing down toward the bottom of the pit. And then he started to swim—or burrow— through the slimy, slithering snakes. Progress was slow, as the snakes were packed in tight, but he soon came to a depth that was relatively calm. Every other snake, it seemed, was dead. Eventually he was digging his way through a mess of snake corpses. He flexed his muscles and kept digging.

When his hands finally touched dirt, he could feel the weight of the snakes like a million sandbags pressing against every inch of his body. He had to calculate each movement carefully in order to bring his body to a horizontal position. He located the tunnel that continued on from the bottom of the pit. Still the tunnel was packed with snake corpses, which seemed nothing more, at this point, than a thick soup of snake guts.

At last, he felt something that was neither dirt nor guts. It was metal. If he could only find some kind of a handle. He did. Pressing down upon the rusted lever with the last of his strength, the door mercifully gave way, and he spilled out into an opening with tile flooring, Persian tapestries on the walls, and neon bulbs hanging down at regular intervals.

Gasping for air as he coughed up a mouthful of snake carcasses, he wiped his eyes clean of sticky guts and looked up to see King X walking up to meet him, all smiles—and two men with machineguns by his side.

110.

Militant King X paced back and forth in front of his snakeskin throne. He held an AK-47 with a gold engraving: "King of Ze Snakes!" A full day had passed since Robbie had faked his death to escape the tunnels. All the while, there hadn't been any word from Eleanor George.

"In ze bast, zat woman, she was calling all of ze time. Now zis. Nozing! Silence! Just when you zink she has a reason to call. She does not. No, I don't like it, Mr. Cox," said King X, wringing the muzzle of his gun as though he were trying to unscrew it.

"Why don't you just call her yourself?" Robbie asked. "Just say you noticed something's up. She'd appreciate that, I'm sure. I mean, I'd call myself if I wasn't supposed to be dead."

"Don't you see? I should have called right away! But I did not! Because I don't know why! Because I was drunk! See? But when I did not call right away, she should have been ze one to call. But she did not. See? Now... Now...!"

"Okay, take it easy, X. She'll call. You can just say you were busy."

"Ah, zat's good. Busy!" he picked up a bottle of rum and raised it in an ironic toast. "Busy drinking ze rum of ze island nations!"

Robbie clinked his glass against King X's bottle. It was no secret that the snake king was a pirate at heart. He had the rum to prove it. Puerto Rican rum stocked by the barrelful.

The rest of the day was spent in heavy drinking. And so was the next day, and the day that followed. The drinking was accompanied by a practically nonstop show of pirate songs and erotic snake dancers.

By the time the afternoon of the fourth day came around, the Militant King X was far too drunk to notice that his top-secret phone line was ringing.

It rang a few times, then stopped. Then started up again. King X began to stir in his drunken slumber, but just then the ringing stopped again.

Robbie was lying beside the king. Halfway into a dream-state, he was thinking: This fucking guy. Calls himself a king. Not so much a king as a con artist superhero with guns and snake pits.

And Robbie thought back on how an excessively drunken X had indulged the truth about his aspirations: "Ze last zing I want is to destroy ze world! Ze world—it is beautiful! Eberywhere, eberywhere it is beautiful blace—but not here. No! Here it is ugly sand foreber and ze burning hot sun. Me, all I want is to take my snakes and mobe to somewhere nice, habing myself ze ocean biew. Eben somewhere in ze woods would be okay wiz snakes in ze trees and rain in ze ribers. But breferably it would be ze beach wiz ze ocean for me!"

Just then the phone rang again. Slipping out of his dream, Robbie reached for the phone and answered it.

"Hello."

"Why have you not called me?" demanded a female voice into his ear. He froze. He knew that voice anywhere. It was George.

"Uh— Ahem! Hm!" Robbie cleared his throat, sitting bolt upright. He was so hung-over it was like his mind had been replaced by a second heart—one made of needles and pounding into every square inch of his head. He reached for the king's rum bottle and took a gulp.

"Are you there? Hello?"

"Yeah, um..." Robbie gathered his wits and sputtered in a thick accent: "It is just ze moment I was about to bick up ze phone and call. It is a most urgent— Uh. Ze most urgent message. Yes, ze damned son of ze beech Robbie Cox...ze politician, has died in ze cabes. Yes, ze snakes has got him."

Robbie held his breath and waited. He took another drink.

"Why didn't you call me sooner?" asked Eleanor George, her tone cold, sterile. "I've seen the video. This happened four days ago."

"Yes. So it seems," said Robbie, holding his forehead and cringing as he spoke. "Zat is ze report as it came to me just now. But ze king has been too busy. Yes, uh, busy drinking ze rum and blanning for ze uh, for ze..."

"For the end of the world," George interjected. "Okay, fine, you idiot. So, Robbie Cox is dead. I only wanted to confirm. We'll discuss the implications later. I need to think. Next time answer the phone immediately when I call. Do you understand?"

"Yes. Answer ze phone immediately. Ze king will do just that—zat, I mean. Just zat"

"Fine. Goodbye."

Robbie set the phone down gently. His head was still throbbing, but the rum seemed to help. He took another drink and looked around the king's underground throne room. Everyone, it seemed—even the snake-dancing girls—was dead ass asleep. There were nine barrels of rum lying empty beside the king's throne. No wonder everyone was passed out: they were absolutely, catatonically wasted.

With a great effort, Robbie came to his feet. So, he thought, George thinks I'm dead. And the Militant King X is a nothing. A totally harmless nobody. It's about time I found my way back to the world. And got back to saving the planet.

111.

You caught that, didn't you? Hopefully it's not too egocentric of me to assume. Everybody's got a right to use their attention as they see fit. I'm a bigtime supporter of freedom of attention. But if I had to bet, I'd say you're already way ahead of me here. You caught the message alright, and you already know what sort of hot water I must have gotten myself into. Well—no kidding!

Hey again, by the way. All of us copyeditors say hello, and all that.

Truth is, when I inserted that little message in italics into the International News and Politics Report, I was really going through a rough spell. Mentally, I mean. Emma called it quits on me. No explanation, either. Totally out of the blue! Possibly it had something to do with the fact that I killed Catwoman. But I'd like to think it was more than that. It's hard to imagine that she felt so much for that damn goldfish.

She stopped coming to the garage. Practically everyone did, as a matter of fact. Now it's primarily just me keeping up the legwork. It's where I've been sleeping lately, so you can understand why I might have become a little obsessive. That's what Emma thinks. Not that she's said that in so many words, but I can read her tone from halfway across the office.

Technically no one knows it was me who wrote that little italicized warning. I've denied it up and down and made up a pretty good story for cover (said there was a strange fellow lurking around the copyeditors' area just before that particular update was scheduled to publish—which was just around the time I left for lunch). Anyway, screw everyone else. Even Emma! I don't care anymore! As if it even matters if they can my ass at this point! Don't they know we're all doomed? Of course they don't!

112.

Interview with a Caucasian landowner, pt. 8: "In Hiding" (WARNING: This interview series is unedited. If you're looking for a break from political correctness and cultural sensitivity, by all means, pull up a plastic spectator chair and enjoy the show!)

INTERVIEWER: Why don't you begin by giving us a recap. Describe where you're at right now and what led up to this point. Tell us how bad it is. That sort of thing.

CAUCASION LANDOWNER: Called out of work for the week. Boss don't gotta know a thing. I just needed some time to think things over. That's all.

I: But you packed up all your belongings, drove three states away, and checked into a motel under a false name. What exactly got you in this situation?

CL: Only one thing you gotta know: Everyone else is at fault here! I'm a saint stuck in a clusterfuck! Okay? Alright?! Life is just like a cockfight sometimes. Where everybody around you is throwing rocks at your cock. First I got a judgment against me in the civil trial brought by the bikini girl for—get this— her hospital bills, her lost wages, her ongoing neck aches and back pains, and the supposed emotional trauma she suffered. In total: a five million dollar judgment. Yeah...right! And then, in the criminal case, the prosecutor went back on his deal. No more plea bargain after I refused to give up my boating license. Told him to go to hell on that one. So he goes for the maximum ten years in prison. Judge is like, hell yeah, can't wait to screw over this poor fucker. Why not. Bam! Ten years. Plus five million in the hole. Just like that. Thanks to that piece of shit bikini girl whose tits you can tell are fake from a mile away and already they're due for an upgrade. No kidding, she should sue her damn plastic surgeon for those tits. Anyway, I don't know. I just had to get the hell away from that situation. And now I'm here.

I: On a scale of one to one-hundred, how would you rate the bed of this one-star motel?

CL: Jeez, man, how the fuck should I know? Seventy-six, maybe? I could sleep on a bed of old car parts, for all I care. A bed's a bed, for Christ's sake.

I: Given the current political climate, do you—

CL: I mean, don't you have any appreciation for how many people don't even have beds, you piece of shit? So many people can't even, uh...

I: Do you always give long speeches when you're drunk like this?

CL: Yes—heh. Yes, sir, I do. And it's good to be drunk. Not a care in the world. Just drunk like a damn...fish.

I: Not that I can blame you.

CL: Yeah, bro. You can say that again, you little prick.

I: So, has the political system let you down? Or do you still have confidence in your representatives to get the job done?

CL: I don't understand the question.

I: Fair enough. All things being equal, would you give up your right to vote for personal happiness?

CL: Happiness as in no debt, more beer? Hell yeah! Where can I sign up for that?

I: Same question, but with freedom of speech.

CL: No debt and beer all the way! Fuck it, anything for money!

I: Anything?

CL: Yeah. And one more thing. A place to spend it all. In a perfect world, with all my money, I'd be able to buy anything I want.

I: That sounds nice.

CL: And live forever.

I: Sure.

113.

No big deal, thought Killian as he entered the bikini rodeo show warehouse.

At his young age, he had a pretty unrealistic idea of what bars were all about. He just assumed they were full of non-stop wickedness and all sorts of incredible, unmentionable things. Like a circus as it should be: with naked girls, daggers flying, guns going off, card games leading to tables overturning, gold-colored alcohol flowing waist-deep as though there were some kind of extreme plumbing problem, and lots and lots of more naked girls along with clothed girls in the process of getting naked.

Once Sweet Jesus disappeared (odd, but maybe just a thing that happens at bars?), Killian accepted a perfect-fitting white bathrobe from an intense man at the entrance.

No big deal, thought Killian.

He walked down the long corridor. Most bars don't have corridors like this one, but Killian didn't know that. At any moment, he was expecting to start slipping, splashing, or swimming in booze. While dodging bullets and fighting off the ladies. But when the hall ended, and he was faced with a door to walk through, his expectations began to fizzle out. An incredibly eerie, hollow-feeling silence crept under the crack beneath the door. Even before he pushed the door open, he knew that he wouldn't find anything but dim lighting and stagnant air on the other side.

It was the ultimate letdown, alright. Just a big, empty warehouse. Nothing to see or do. That was the shape of things. All except for the nearest corner of the warehouse, which had a bar, at least. Also some couches, a piano, and a pool table.

A man in a white suit leaned against the bar. He held a drink in his hand, twirling it casually as if it were a gun he might like to shoot, for no other reason than to look fancy. He took a sip.

"Hello, Killian," said the man.

Killian blinked. It quickly sunk in that the entire situation had to be recalculated. Even the hollow-feeling silence was suddenly not what it seemed.

Hello, Meriwether, thought Killian without moving his lips. In the back of his mind he remembered, must defeat Dudebuddy. The thought made his breath shallow, his legs nearly paralyzed.

"Come over here. Glad you could make it. Sorry this place is so…you know…drab."

Killian walked over to the nearest couch but didn't sit.

"Fantastic-looking bathrobe you got there, by the way. You remember me, right? The man you don't quite understand? The guy from your dreams?"

"Yeah."

"Okay, good! I'm a superhero, too, you know. If you need a reason to feel better about leaving old Sweet Jesus behind. I'm just a superhero of a different ilk. No one votes for me to keep me going, for instance. I just have my role and I do it. And I do it very well, I might add."

Meriwether finished his drink and slammed the glass down on the bar. He stood up, straightening his white tie and the lapels of his white suit.

"Alright, I'm officially over this place. Look at it. We've got this whole glorious universe, yet this damn warehouse in Arkansas ends up being the portal to the enlightened plane. Go figure, huh? Supposedly it's the least political point in your little cosmos. Guess that's the problem, at its heart, really. All the good places, like Big Sur or Leicester Square, are all so grossly infected with politics. But whatever. Let's get out of here. How do you feel about going to the beach? I got a thing for the beach scene. Let's go to the beach."

114.

The beach. Wow, too much for a moment—you almost had to stand back with your arms over your face and your eyes closed, it was so bright. But then it was A-okay. The leisurely, neon blue wave that sauntered up to the shoreline said it all. It just sat there enjoying itself, having a little indulgence party, wondering about the tiny bits of sand, if they'd like a saltwater bath, and then giving it to them. And the palm trees with their shadows said it too. Aloha. Welcome to some strange kind of untouchable fantasy land.

Down the shoreline a short distance, a girl in a swimsuit and a summer hat was walking along like the first thing you'd think to insert into a dream. Even before he could bring his eyes into focus, he knew it was Jenny.

"What's she doing here?" asked Killian.

"Don't you think it's better this way?" said Meriwether. "With everything working out in the end?"

Meriwether made introductions. "But I guess you already know each other," he said.

Killian dug one foot into the sand, unsure how to act, and scowled at Jenny. She smiled at him and said, "Jeez, I've been waiting a long time!"

"Speaking of which, I gotta go," said Meriwether, talking fast. "Sorry to— Hah! No need to jabber on, at this point. Alright, have fun! See you—!"

And just like that, he was gone.

"Come on," said Jenny.

A memory flashed into Killian's mind. Something about a warehouse. Walking into a warehouse, wearing a white robe. Sweet Jesus... Or was that just all a dream?

"Where are we going?"

"Out of the sun. It's too hot!"

It was true. Killian hadn't noticed until then, but the sand was scorching under his bare feet. Also he noticed that he was wearing tropical shorts and no shirt; and the sun was beginning to fry his bare skin.

She led him toward a grove of palm trees at the edge of a jungle oasis. They walked fast, kicking their feet against the sand so it wouldn't burn so much.

"Hey," Killian asked suddenly, "are you real?"

"What's that supposed to mean?"

"Well we hardly spoke, really, in Ms. Buckingham's class, so I never even knew what you thought about me. And then in my dream the other night—" he broke off. Those moments from his dream were too intimate to mention out loud.

"Yeah, I know. But it's different now. Now I can't even remember much from before. It's like I've been here forever. Sorry if I appeared in your dream, or whatever. Sometimes that's just what happens, I guess."

Killian thought this over. Meanwhile, the grove of palm trees didn't seem to be getting any closer.

"Wait," he said. "What is this place?"

"You'll see!"

115.

INTERNATIONAL NEWS AND POLITICS REPORT: Robbie Cox mysteriously appeared—back from the dead?—just in time to save the planet from an impending asteroid impact. NASA warns the impact will likely occur in three weeks and counting. The point of impact is estimated to be somewhere in the northern hemisphere. Unless diverted, it could very likely decimate a landmass the size of Europe. According to NASA officials, the sudden appearance of Robbie Cox has brought a healthy sense of optimism. Nonetheless, without adequate funding from the appropriate political channels, it's feared that even Robbie Cox won't be of any meaningful service. Etc. Etc. Etc.

Note: *Hey, so, it's the copyeditors again and we've gotta say we're not surprised at all. Not one bit! It's the DLF! Why won't somebody freaking do something already? It's just really, really frustrating to be one of the little guys. Watching this all unfold. And not being able to do shit about it. Know what's next? Global nuclear war. Then artificial superintelligence turning against all biological life. Then an apocalyptic terrorist uprising. It's all written out. It's all right there! All part of Dudebuddy's plan and he's been planning it for centuries! Come on. Do something to stop him already! Okay, that's all.*

116.

POLITICAL OP-ED: Sad to say, the headlines are true. This is our last publication. Eleanor George, our fearless leader of all things media, has determined that we are no longer fit to continue on as a publication. Tomorrow, the world will wake up with no International News and Politics Report for the first time since the turn of the century. And my humble Political Op-Ed section is going down with the ship. ALL BECAUSE SOME JACKASS IN THE COPYEDITOR'S DEPARTMENT DECIDED TO RANT ABOUT HIS CRAZY BATSHIT CONSPIRACY THEORY!

The DLF, he says. ...Right! As if that's anything but a kids' fairytale. As if the modern world is seriously threatened by a bunch of guys in bathrobes!

You know what? I hope he's right. I hope the big, bad DLF is behind Erectalphlegm Syndrome, the giant virus allegedly plaguing the world, and the asteroid. Also, I hope they're the reason Eleanor George has apparently decided to do almost nothing about rounding up the troops to stop these disasters. Because that would just serve him right if the DLF comes and destroys the world!

In the meantime, all signs indicate otherwise. It's a beautiful day outside. No diseases or asteroids on the wind, in the forecast, or creeping over my shoulder today. So, I'll be taking my unemployment to the great outdoors. I'll be the guy catching fish, keeping my opinions bottled up like the way I'm holding back my true feelings right now about THAT JACKASS. If anyone needs any opinions of a political kind, I'm sure you can find plenty in the evening cartoons.

117.

"Anarchy is the natural state of things," said Al to Trista, who was driving him and Charlie to the airport. Al had saved up just enough cash to buy two plane tickets. Charlie was asleep in the backseat. He'd been taking sleeping pills and likely had no idea what was happening.

"Yeah, how so?" asked Trista in a snooty tone. She still had a superiority complex about her beliefs in the democratic process of electing superheroes.

"Just think about this," said Al. "Anarchy is a society without any recognized authority. There's one basic problem to this, which is that, in a state without formal lawmakers, the rules will always end up being made by the bullies. Sometimes those bullies come to power one way, and sometimes they come to power another way. Sometimes it's through democracy, sometimes through monarchy. But it's always anarchy underneath it all. Whether you live in a democratic society or a monarchy, you still live in a state of anarchy, just with a different type of bully making the rules."

"At least with democracy, you get to pick your bullies."

"Possibly in a sense. But you only get to vote because the bullies say you get to. Tomorrow, they could change their mind and say you can't vote anymore. Then what are you going to do—revolt? Then you're the bully. See what I mean? Underneath, it's always anarchy."

Trista was silent as she turned off toward the airport terminal. But then she said, "I'm over it. All this talk just makes me want to be apolitical."

There was a scream from the backseat: "Apolitical? Where the hell did you get a goddamn silly idea like that?!"

Charlie's head poked into the front of the car, his gold crown pulled halfway down over his eyes. "And where the hell are you taking me?"

118.

Dr. Gilbert sat at his lab table, just as he'd been sitting for days and days, like an overworked lab rat. It was long past normal hours, and the only light on in the place was his table light. The rest of the lab was smothered in darkness, with steampunk-looking shadows stretched out over the metal tables all the way to the green exit sign glowing in the far corner.

The vials cluttering up his elbow space were labeled things like:

SUPER LETHAL

LETHAL FOR SMALL CHILDREN
LEGAL IN LARGE DOSES
MOST CONTAGIOS BUT NONLETHAL
PLAIN ARSNIC

And RUBBING ALCOHOL. There was also one vial marked ANTIDOTE (?), which was empty.

There was no antidote. Not without Killian.

After staring at the empty vial for some time, Dr. Gilbert's eyes lowered. He looked down at his hand resting on the table. His pointer finger twitched. And there, on the side of his finger, was a small, fresh cut, as if it had recently scraped against a piece of sharp glass. A drop of blood had formed; as he lifted his finger, the drop of blood slipped around the crease and ran down into his palm. He watched it slowly dry.

119.

Killian felt like he must have been walking across hot sand for an eternity. But his sense of time was seriously warped. The palm trees never seemed to get any closer.

He called out to Jenny to stop. To wait up! But she just kept skipping on ahead. How many times had he called out to her? He couldn't even imagine. Hundreds of times? Thousands?

The heat grew so intense that the edges of his vision began to blur and fade into blackness. The vibrant world of gold sand, blue sky, and distant palms all began to disintegrate into darkness.

Hours or maybe days later, Killian was still walking across the beach sand. But the sun no longer bothered him and he'd forgotten all about Jenny. She had not only disappeared from sight, but from memory.

Next thing he knew, he woke up in some sort of tropical

hut. The walls were made of colorful driftwood; the thatched roof was rustic and casual, as if an ocean breeze had placed the dried palm leaves that way. Sitting up, he swayed back and forth mysteriously for a few moments before realizing he was in a hammock.

Nothing made sense... What was this place? Was he on vacation? Was he shipwrecked?

Carefully, Killian pulled open the door of the hut. He peaked outside. It was an idyllic beach scene. Palm trees all around, tables set with pitchers of tropical drinks, waves rolling up on the nearby shore, a cloud or two drifting across the horizon.

"Hey, Dudebuddy!"

Killian almost jumped. He pushed the door open wider and saw a man sitting at one of the tables. Despite the man's white beard that grew halfway down his bare chest, he appeared youthful and vigorous. He was tan, muscular, and glowing with life.

"Welcome to Dudebuddy Nation!" said the man, smiling wilding and raising a cherry-red cocktail in greeting. "Pull up a seat. I'll pour you a drink."

Killian's first thought was, wait, I'm too young to drink. But the next moment he was taking a big sip of a delicious, fruity beverage as if it were the most natural thing to do in the morning. His reflection flashed in the glass: in fact, it wasn't a child's face he saw reflected; but it wasn't exactly an adult's face, either. It was like he was something new and ageless.

"Not bad, huh?" said the man. "It's coconut, strawberry, lime, rum, ice. Sometimes I swap out the strawberry with mango or more coconut. Or more lime."

"It's—wow... Really good."

"Hah, hah! Come on, take a seat, Dudebuddy."

Killian accepted the invitation. Thinking out loud, he said, "Dudebuddy?"

"That's right. I'm Dudebuddy. You're Dudebuddy. We're all Dudebuddy! Everybody's Dudebuddy in Dudebuddy Nation!"

Killian took another drink. A calming, almost tranquilizing sort of happiness spread throughout his body. He couldn't tell if he was breathing in deep or letting out the biggest sigh of his life. But he sunk into the straw chair and every care in the world flitted away. Except for one thought.

"I don't remember..." he began, but just as quickly lost the thought. He tried again. "How...how did I get here?"

"Hah, hah! I wouldn't worry too much about that. Unless you want to hear a long and dull story about pirates and I don't even know what else in terms of the physics. Believe me, I wouldn't worry about it. Dudebuddy Nation is the place to say, 'Eh? Somebody say worry? Worry? I don't see any worries. Do you?' —Hah! That's about all there is to it."

Killian found himself laughing right along with Dudebuddy. The guy was, for some reason—something about his comical voice and his crazy, carefree air—absolutely hilarious.

"Anyway, anyway, hah! Let's just say this. We'll just, you know, do a side little wheel and deal with whatever might have happened and let's just say a pirate dropped you off on this here seashore—and now?" Dudebuddy raised his hands, exaggerating the point, "And now you're here! Hah, hah!"

"Okay—yeah, yeah," Killian agreed, smiling, happy to have that settled.

"More drink? Good, huh?! Sure—alright!"

120.

After an incredibly long and uneventful night at the bikini rodeo show, Sweet Jesus realized with mixed emotions that closing time had finally come. Still no sign of Killian's return—no sign of anything beyond this immediate world of meatheads and bikini girls.

The entire night, Sweet Jesus had kept himself incognito by huddling over his drink and never mentioning a word about politics. But even so he had the feeling that he was being watched.

Well, I'll give them something to watch, he thought. It was a drunken thought, and a tired thought, but it helped him feel better about his long night's worth of agitation.

There was a TV remote control left unattended on the bar. He swooped it up. All night, the TVs over the bar had been playing nothing but sports. Now that the remote was in his hands, he would change that. Get ready to be infiltrated by some politics, he thought. It was the first uplifting thought he'd had all evening.

What would they do? he wondered. Would they freak out? Had these meathead Arkansas locals ever even seen a political news broadcast before?

He began flipping through the channels. At first, no luck. Just more sports. Dudes hitting baseballs. Dudes racing cars. Dudes throwing footballs and hitting each other. He kept flipping and still—no luck. An eerie tingle crept down Sweet Jesus's spine. He knew Arkansans had a natural disinclination toward politics, but were they also actively sheltered from exposure to anything beyond sports, beer, and bikini bull riding?

Perhaps there was still one last way to find out. Reaching deep into his pants pocket, he pulled out the Sovereign Summons, that ancient, mythical text, now crumpled and stained nearly beyond recognition. Sitting there on his wobbly stool under blaring sports broadcasts, he read the incantation in full. It was a desperate thing to do, he realized. And brash. The incantation had—for all he knew—never been read before. Anything could happen. Something earth-shattering, even.

"Last call, old timer," said the bartender, just as Sweet Jesus muttered the final passage. "Need another?"

Ignoring the bartender, Sweet Jesus glared at the ancient text, waiting, hoping. Finally he laid it on the bar, crumpling it up like a napkin ready for the trash.

With a sigh, he flipped the television off, shook his head, and quietly joined the crowd of meatheads on their way out.

121.

Feeling trapped. Worse than that, it's not just a feeling. If it were, I'd just say to myself, get over it, stupid. You're okay. It's just a rough patch. Think positive thoughts and blast triumphant songs like you're at a sports rally with cheerleaders screaming your name if that helps. But—ah, hah. It's not just some feeling to get over. I'm trapped for real. Trapped!

Anybody out there need copyeditor services? That's a joke, of course. The world is going to end at any moment, at this point. So the last thing anybody should be doing is worrying about copyediting. But it would be nice to have some work to distract myself with these final days.

Been holed up in the garage. Bleary-eyed and surrounded by a world of comic book clippings. And a mountain of beer cases and other provisions. Also a gigantic picture of Alalia I printed out. Still not sure how she figures into all of this. Unless she's the reincarnated version of Eleanor George. Which at this point wouldn't surprise me one bit.

All this time, it's been my one fear that the bathrobe-wearing guys will come. The DLF. But now I say. Let them come. I'm ready. Among other things, ready for treason. Ready to switch sides. I've already lost my livelihood so why the hell not. Now all I've got is my relative youth and this mountain of beer. So come on and take me already. Sure, I'll join up. I'll go to the Dudebuddy.

Dudebuddy, Dudebuddy, Dudebuddy. Maybe if I say his name he'll come. Except I know that's not how it works. You've got to dream. He'll come into your dreams. And tell you thanks for believing in the Dudebuddy jive. I'll never let you down. Come on. Come to me. Join my team. It's all anarchy everywhere anyway. You know it is. Come on, etc. And then next thing I'll be one of them. Holding up a sign. In a white bathrobe like I'm getting ready for a minor role in a sleazy film. Liberate Dudebuddy.

But you have to forgive me for these thoughts. I'm not well. I've been coughing. I've been feverish as hell. I keep pacing back and forth between the beer mountain and Alalia. Thinking, am I about to keel over? Is this the plague? Is the sickness turning my bloodstream black and derailing my better judgment? Is it too late for me? Me, the last of the faithful copyeditors?

122.

Robbie Cox in broad daylight strolled down the sidewalk of a nondescript suburban neighborhood. As though canvassing for votes. He was dressed in a slim-fitting dress shirt with the sleeves rolled up. His hair coifed. His muscles flexed. His look said: Let's do this, whatever it is, it don't matter.

He stopped at a tan, one-story house with a cracked driveway and weeds overtaking the lawn. His look said: This is the place, as he took out a piece of gum and chomped it casually with his back teeth.

He walked down the driveway, then around to the side of the garage. There was a window and a door. He didn't bother to peak inside. Instead, in one perfectly executed movement, he kicked down the door. It went flying off its hinges.

There was a short scream from inside. Followed by a terrified: "Oh, shit!"

Stepping onto the fallen door, Robbie glanced around the chaotic mess of the garage. At first glance, the place was nothing but a sea of beer cans and comic books.

Also there was a young guy—perhaps late twenties—in jeans and an unbuttoned collared shirt looking bug-eyed and wild. The guy had apparently attempted to hide behind a stack of beer cases, but his body didn't nearly fit. Realizing it was a lost cause, he just stared back at Robbie in a state of confused, half-drunken fear.

"Hey champ," said Robbie, standing tall with his fists locked onto hips, as if he were ready for a superhero photoshoot. "You the guy who wrote those italicized remarks about the Dudebuddy Liberation Front?"

"Yeah..." said the guy, slowly coming to his feet.

"A copyeditor, right?"

"Yes, sir."

"I'm Robbie Cox. I used to read the International News and Politics Report everyday. Sometimes it was about me. Whenever I made a headline, I'd save it in a special folder. Don't know why. Guess it was just a way to keep track of my life, like a diary, and also stay up on the latest international news at the same time. It's a shame what happened."

"I didn't mean for that!" said the copyeditor, panicking. "I just— I thought when I— I mean, I had no idea they would cancel the whole publication!"

Robbie Cox stepped closer. He picked up a stray beer and cracked it open.

"Have the people in the white bathrobes been here yet?"

"I'm not sure. I don't think so."

"They'll come after you. I'm surprised they haven't already."

"What should I do?"

"Listen," he said, taking a drink. "I need you to tell me everything you know."

123.

Interview with a Caucasian landowner, pt. 9: "Best Case Scenario" (WARNING: This interview series is unedited. If you find your spiritual journey damaged in any way, shape, or form by the following text, just know you've been warned upfront. Also, as you gather up the shreds of your journey and begin again with an open heart, take solace in the fact that you aren't alone: we've been damaged, too.)

INTERVIEWER: Best case scenario, you get out of here alive, you get a new name, you start a new life.

CAUCASIAN LANDOWNER: No, best case scenario, everyone forgets the whole thing and I go back to life as usual. I didn't ask for this, man!

I: Yet, the world could end at any moment, and you're worried about—

CL: I don't give a shit! Everything that's ever happened to me is so totally bogus! You know what? I say fuck you, man. Fuck you, fuck my lawyer, fuck the girl in my boat in the bikini with fake tits, fuck the government and the property taxes I have to pay... You know? God!

I: But still you're a full-fledged Caucasian. So you have that. And you're a landowner.

CL: Since the age of twenty-three! Damn right!

I: What were you before that?

CL: I rented. I was a Caucasian renter.

I: One bedroom or studio?

CL: Studio. A big studio. Don't remember the exact square footage but you might as well call it a one bedroom, really. Had its own balcony and a parking space. Also lived with a girl once in a duplex. But she was crazy. That place was a dump. Went from there to living in my truck for a couple months. I swear, those were my best days. Unemployed and living off beer I'd steal from gas stations.

I: A Caucasian beer thief.

CL: I'd just park someplace, you know, where no one would bother me. Out by the city dump, or wherever. All day long I'd just sit there in the truck bed chugging down beer. I had a tarp, even, for when it rained.

I: So, what happened?

CL: Then I just got this job in construction. My dad hooked me up with some work at his company, actually. He helped me out with the down payment for my house. So I wouldn't have to, you know, keep on paying rent like some kind of bottom dweller. I was only twenty-three!

I: Pretty heroic, I guess. Caucasian superhero over here.

CL: You know it!

124.

POLITICAL OP-ED: Guess what... I'm back! That's right! First, I'd like to give a big thanks to Country Homemakers Magazine for serving as the new platform for my political commentary. The International News and Politics Report may be deceased, but not me. I've still got a few things to say. You can be sure about that!

All my loyal readers can rest assured I'll pick up right where I left off. And to all you Country Homemaker fans out there, let me tell you right up front that this may not be for you. Just flip right on by to find your apple pie recipes, your goat milking tips, or whatever it is you read this silly publication for.

Jumping right back to it. Damn it feels good to have my column back! And it's not a moment too soon! A lot has happened! Today, I'll zero in on the muckiest of the muck with a recap of what's been going on:

1) Erectalphlegm Syndrome is now killing off sections of Asia, Africa, and Eastern Europe and picking up speed. It's only a matter of time before the orange-tinted toxic phlegm sparks a nuclear reaction that may kill millions in one blow.

2) The mysterious giant virus out of North America that's apparently factory produced is causing full towns, one after another, to be turned into mass burial sites. Although, that's still speculation. Who the heck knows, ladies!

3) The impending asteroid impact is expected to collide into the northern hemisphere in a matter of weeks. Barring some miracle, the asteroid will have its pick between destroy-

ing either all of Europe or the continental United States.

So, that's what's on the menu. Sounds like a great show to me, if ever there was one! Somebody's got a job to do, that's for sure! Now's the time, superheroes!

I do enjoy a good challenge. And three cheers, Eleanor George, for leading us on with the suspense. If the politicians don't do something soon, we'll all be toast! Hah!

Speaking of which, what's next? If I remember this year's list correctly, I believe we still have global nuclear war and an apocalyptic terrorist uprising to look forward to.

Meanwhile, some wackjob out there is still thinking... DLF! Now, that's the real tragedy. Mental illness. So sad. Am I bitter? Maybe. Anyway, who's up for some apple pie recipes? How about today's top gardening tips? Also I've got all these mason jars and I just don't know what to put in them... Help! Ha! Ha! Ha!

125.

A spaceship landing. Right there on the beach. Casting multi-colored lights. Also millions of tiny tornadoes, as if to make the sand play tickle torture with itself. What was this— some kind of cartoon show?

Meriwether: Sloppy the way it handles its gravity if you ask me, but otherwise a smooth ride.

Eleanor George: Sleeping accommodations, however...

Meriwether: Oh, psh!

Time still off, still not quite right, Killian thought, glancing at Eleanor and Meriwether, then at the spaceship. He wondered what might have happened in between the moment it landed and now. Dudebuddy, laughing nonstop, poured drinks for days.

Meriwether: It's still dreamlike for the kid, alright. Just look at him. Good drinks, huh kid? Yeah? Huh? Hah! You know when I dropped him off at the shoreline—

Eleanor: Which, I can't believe—

Dudebuddy: Ha! Ha!

Meriwether: When I dropped him off, I found him that girl he dreams about. The one from his class. Thought she might stick it out. Wasn't sure. Guess not.

Dudebuddy: Hot damn, almost didn't think about that. When he trotted up here from the beach, it could have felt like an absolute eternity.

Eleanor: He very well may not have made it.

Meriwether: Yeah, hence the girl. Knew she'd help him make it! Pretty good test in my book.

Killian was grinning at everything, sloshing down the drinks. Each gulp had a calming, cooling effect, almost like the opposite of getting drunk. He felt drunk, but the drinks, some-how, seemed to bring everything further into clarity. If only he could keep drinking. Maybe down a couple more pitchers. Then maybe he'd get his sense of time back.

Dudebuddy: He must have had some pretty good dreams about her. Bet she's pretty!

Meriwether: Sure! Just his type, too. You still remember her, kid? From your dreams? See, dreams and alternate di-mensions—there's a little bit of overlap. You pass into a new dimension, you can take some of your dreams right along for the ride. With the right touch, you can even make them come to life.

"I remember," said Killian, sort of half-grinning.

Others were walking about in beach clothes or no clothes at all. Calling out to Dudebuddy and laughing, calling each other Dudebuddy. Would the sun ever set? Maybe it did already and then came back up again? Was it always this hard to tell? Strange thoughts to be having. Couldn't say that they were disturbing exactly. Just a little strange, was all.

Comradery. That was the predominant feeling. Above all else was this feeling of comradery. Drinking up and feeling the presence of everyone, even complete strangers, as if they were your favorite things to hug. Big, loving stuffed critters. Talking, laughing, having a good time on the beach under palm tree shade.

Eleanor: I just got so sick of politics.

Killian thought, just barely keeping it to himself: Wow, even she's lightening up!

Eleanor: All the spectacle and the game of it all. Having to justify it all. As though it weren't obviously about the marketing. As though the marketing existed independent of the show.

Meriwether patted Dudebuddy on the back. The word "politics" seemed to be a lot for him to take.

Eleanor: But then Meriwether gave me a chance to get out of it. When I didn't even know there was an out. There was an open position as Secretary of Interstellar Space Stations.

Meriwether: Interstellar and interdimensional.

Eleanor: First I had those dreams.

Dudebuddy: Pretty great, yeah? I just think they're so good! Don't know why everybody doesn't like them.

Meriwether, shaking his head: Some people... It's pathetic, really. Not open to new experiences or even the thought of something better!

Eleanor: But I said yes. Sign me up.

Killian: What happened to the former secretary?

Dudebuddy laughed but Meriwether for the first time took on a serious look.

Meriwether: There was no former secretary. There were certain prophesies, but that's not so unusual. Time and space are easy enough to see through. It's no wonder prophesies should exist. But they're never fully right. You might say that prophesies are only the cartoon versions of the reality to come.

The stars came out. There were half a dozen moons in the sky. After hundreds or possibly thousands of drinks, it was finally time to call it a day.

126.

Uncle Jon in his lab coat appeared out of nowhere in the middle of an ocean under a starless night sky. He popped to the surface like tearing his way out of a showroom full of ultra-soft but suffocating black sheets. But then his struggle was over. He pulled himself up on his elbows, wiggled his knees out of the dark slosh, and a moment later sat on top of the water's surface. As if the ocean which might have been bottomless, did have a top.

He said, "Killian...! Killian...!"

"I'm here."

"What?!"

"I said, 'I'm here.'"

"Where?"

"I don't know. But you're right there. Sitting on the ocean."

"Okay. It's a weird place. I think it may not be anywhere. But I'll just assume you can hear me."

"I can. What's going on, Uncle Jon?"

"Well, first, I think I died. I cut myself in the lab; I became infected. With my own virus. And now I'm here. That's all I know. —Oh, wait! That's not all. I came here to tell you something. Something important. Let me think."

"Is it about Jenny?"

"Jenny? Who's Jenny?"

"She's— Never mind, I guess."

"Ah, ah, I remember now! It's you. You're the cure for the virus. I gave you a shot into your bloodstream of the antidote to all strains. Even to Erectalphlegm Syndrom, just in case. Even though that's a silly, going-nowhere virus if you ask me. Mostly a scare tactic. Nothing compared to the infectious nightmare I created. Which is why I couldn't help creating an antidote. And there was only one place I could think to hide it. In the bloodstream of someone who had already been infected, so they'd already have the antibodies. And that's you. You're the only hope to save the world!"

The water sloshed against Uncle Jon's body. He tried to stand, but then decided against it. He repositioned himself and looked around at the nebulous distance on all sides.

"Hello?" he called. "Are you still there?"

"Yeah, I'm still here."

"Okay. Wherever you are—you know what to do!"

"But what if..."

"Nothing to worry about! I have full confidence in you!"

"But what if it's best for the world to end, you know?"

"It's not!" Uncle Jon shouted. "Or you know what, maybe it is. I don't know! I believed in Dudebuddy for so long. I followed Dudebuddy for so long. I thought it was something important. For once, something bigger than politics, bigger than superheroes. I couldn't tell you how sick I was of superheroes always solving every problem. I wanted science to do that! For that matter, I wanted to do that! So when Dudebuddy came into my dreams and said he'd end politics forever, I had to get in on that. Something bigger than politics? A world with no politics at all? I said alright! Finally I can help solve a problem! But now I don't know. I feel like I've been used. And I'm not so sure if I ever knew what I was signing up for. Anyway I don't feel as enthusiastic about it as I used to. And now I'm dead, apparently. Oh, great..."

The water had risen quickly. It was up to his torso, sloshing up to his chest. In a panic, he turned and began to crawl, as if hoping he might find something to crawl onto. He tried to stand and only sank further. Soon he was flailing in his lab coat, half swimming... He let out a cry, but his voice didn't carry. And then, as if pulled under, he vanished.

127.

Robbie Cox, down on his hands and knees, peaked underneath the garage door. "They're here," he said.

"I'm almost done," said the copyeditor, frantically taping shut a box.

The garage had been completely cleaned up. No more comic book clippings hanging from the walls, the ceiling, or scattered around on the floor. The beer cases had been stacked neatly and pushed to one side, like a modest wall of beer. It looked pretty much like a normal suburban garage again.

"Take your time," said Robbie, coming to his feet.

"There's one more thing," said the copyeditor. "Something I didn't mention..."

"Sure. What's that?"

"I've been having dreams—the dreams. The ones about how, uh— You know, 'Liberate Dudebuddy' and all that."

"I wouldn't worry about it."

"But they're awfully convincing."

"So, what? You want to go destroy the world, too?"

"No. But..."

"Hold it together, man. You know what I dreamed about last night?"

"What?"

"My one true absolute love abandoning me and feeding me piece by piece to a pit of stakes. Last of all my head. My whole head tossed down into a snake pit and swallowed up like a gum drop. The same head still in love with her. Inside the belly of a snake, still in love and thinking, 'Yeah, but, isn't she still so wonderful?' That's what dreams are, man. Nonsensical episodes that are even more absurd for the fact that they seem to have a sense of cause and effect. When, really, it's just a garbage dump of thoughts."

"Jeez, I never knew a superhero could be so cynical."

"Disappointed? I guess that's a sign of the times. Okay. Ready?"

The copyeditor looked up, startled. "What about— I thought you said they were out there? Shouldn't we wait?"

"No. No time. They could be there for days."

"But what's going to happen?"

"Right this moment, the world as we know it is crumbling all around us," said Robbie, picking up an armful of boxes. "Otherwise, nothing to worry about."

The copyeditor followed Robbie Cox out the side door. They

both carried a number of boxes in their arms, plus a few cases of beer. Across the street, sure enough, there stood a group of the white bathrobe-wearing guys. Holding the proverbial signs. Liberate Dudebuddy.

Robbie kept a sturdy strut as he walked down the driveway, turned, and kept on going at a good clip down the sidewalk. The copyeditor, following closely on Robbie's heels, couldn't help it and cast a neighborly smile at the stoic crew of sign-holders. He even nodded his head hello. Then he gulped and rushed ahead to Robbie's car, where he buckled himself into the front seat and ducked down as they drove away, just hoping he hadn't slipped up and accidentally lost his soul to those things he'd just seen, the same things he dreamed about every night, those anarchist aliens.

128.

Just when all these cartoon reruns were getting so stale and downright blah, FINALLY there's something new to watch! So, get ready! Are you ready yet? NOW are you ready? Okay! You better be, because this is the cartoon show you've been waiting for!

Introducing a brand new superhero! He's not only a super cool guy, he's also the youngest superhero possibly ever in the history of superheroes. His name? Killian Gladstone!

He's just back this moment from the mysterious land of Dudebuddy Nation—the land of no politics. But, like, HUH? The land of no wha—? Yeah! THAT!

That's right: it's a new thing! A superhero who's actually AGAINST politics. Even this, right now, this cartoon. NOT politics. All these flashing colors and this peppy musical tune and this killer beat—guess what, NOT politics!

Plus, you get to wear a cool bathrobe. Seriously, cool bathrobe, huh? It's almost like everyone's wearing one these days. You noticed that? Almost as if like there must be something to it! And guess what! Just like you thought! There is!

Here's Killian in a bathrobe shaking hands with Eleanor George.

Here's Killian in a bathrobe on top of the world's tallest building with his hands on his hips looking out over pretty much everything.

Here's Killian more regal than ever in a bathrobe riding bareback on a horse. Scratch that, a stallion!

Here he is off-boarding in a bathrobe from a private jet, visiting some poor, sick nation with Erectalphlegm Syndrome obliterating dudes left and right (awkward).

And here he is in George's London penthouse office, making plans for the future, at the top of his game, not a care in the world, in a bathrobe!

129.

Back in the desert, struck suddenly with a terrible craving for all things that slither and hiss. But nearly dying of thirst and also sensing that time was quickly running out for the world, Robbie ignored his hunger. He carried the passed-out and possibly dead copyeditor over his shoulder.

First their plane went down. Then a posse of desert thieves had attacked with swords. The thieves saw right away that neither Robbie nor his companion carried anything resembling valuables, but still they wanted a swordfight.

"Are you not man enough?!" they hollered in some language

Robbie couldn't comprehend.

"Come on, bro," said Robbie, frustrated, "just let us wander off into the middle of the desert already. I know you can't understand me, but at some basic human level you've got to hear in the tone of my voice that we mean you no harm, that we appreciate you not getting all up in our shit, and that you have no idea who the hell you're dealing with."

Someone made the first move and then a bunch of swords clashed together until finally Robbie stood on top of a pile of dead thieves' bodies. He had to yank the copyeditor out from under the pile of bodies, as if the guy had been hiding under there for a sense of security and didn't want to leave.

Then, walking deeper and deeper into the middle of the desert, Robbie was faced with having no idea how to find his way back to the uncharted dunes. At least he had a sword now, sharpened and ready for battle, which he'd taken off the body of the leader of the thieves. But what he really needed was a compass. And a photographic memory of how to find his way back to the middle of nowhere.

Then, two days into wandering around under the desert sun, he heard a distinctive hissing sound. It could very well have been a figment of his imagination, but in any case he was struck with a hunger for that scaly flesh.

"When you're looking for the king of the snakes," Robbie said to the copyeditor, "you follow the sound of the snakes."

The copyeditor was already passed out by this time, but talking to his lifeless form was somehow better than talking to oneself. Over the next few days, Robbie told the lifeless form all of his most personal secrets—the types of things he'd never told anyone before and would never tell again. Mostly about

Eleanor George. And how he felt deeply betrayed. And how at this point he wouldn't mind seeing her disgraced.

But then Robbie grew silent. His attention was fully drawn to an underground sea of slithering, hissing sounds, and the feeling of his own overly-dry mouth salivating for the first time since the plane crash.

And that's when he knew he'd finally arrived. Back at the terrorist-harboring caves in the uncharted dunes. And this time he had a pretty good idea how to find the front door. Minutes later, he was walking down a long corridor of Militant King X's secret underground palace.

130.

Interview with a Caucasian landowner, pt. 9: "Rebirth" (WARNING: This interview series is unedited. It's very close in nature to your own deepest, darkest thoughts, in fact. As God is your witness, fess up.)

INTERVIEWER: How's the fit?

CAUCASIAN LANDOWNER: Loose and flowing. Like freedom, my favorite kind: easy on the balls.

I: Any second thoughts about abandoning your countrymen in their spiritual fight against this form of evil you now embody in this bathrobe?

CL: Bro, I ain't got time for second thoughts. I'm a new man!

I: At least you don't shy away from making decisions out of desperation, I see.

CL: I got two words. Liberate Dudebuddy, you bitch.

I: Do you actually believe? Or did you just join up because you're running away scared from your troubles?

CL: Psh. Belief is for old ladies.

I: What about old lady nihilists?

CL: Ha, ha! This fuckin' guy!

I: ...Ready? Here he comes.

CL: Just, uh—just shut the hell up. I'll do the talking.

MERIWETHER: Hey there! You must be one of the newbies.

CL: Yep... Yep...

M: When was the last time you voted?

CL: Like for an election? Never!

M: Really? Wow. Not even—

CL: Nah. Just seemed kinda like the ultimate feel-good sport for the weak. So long as I've got football and beer, who gives a shit, you know? And there's always gonna be that!

M: Hah! Sure! Okay, bud, you're alright. Here's a drink for ya. Drink up. And when you're done, free refills. Keep drinking. Don't stop.

CL: Hell yeah, that's what I like to hear.

M: Great. Carry on!

CL: Fuck yeah! Ha, ha!

I: Is that true?

CL: What?

I: That you've never voted?

CL: Maybe. Shit, I don't know. It's not like I ever really cared, even if I did. Same difference, or whatever.

I: So the world ending is now pretty much your main pre-rogative? Your property ownership rights be damned, even?

CL: What the hell. I don't know, man. You trying to make me nervous or something?

I: How's the drink?

CL: Not bad!

I: The guy was pretty nice.

CL: You heard what he said? Free refills!

131.

Leaning back in his snakeskin throne, spiced rum dripping off his lips, the Militant King X had his own ideas of what should happen next.

"Ze world is ending. Ze baz-robe idiots can take it. Fuck ze world. It is dead to me."

It was clear that he had thought a lot about this. Also, apparently he had not stopped drinking "ze rum of ze island nations" since Robbie Cox had made his escape weeks ago.

"First," said King X, explaining himself, "first ze asteroid will come and destroy ze whole of Eurobe. Zen, zat catastrophe will cause ze beginning of ze global nuclear war. Zen, ze artificial suberintelligence will turn against all life in ze world. Zen, ze terrorists will rise ub in mass force. Zen, ze rogue black hole—"

"You're just quoting the list of apocalyptic shit put together at the world leaders' conference," said Robbie, not impressed.

The copyeditor, now fully revived and sipping bottled water, kept quiet.

"But it's true! It's all habbening! One zing, zen ze next!"

"Maybe so, X," said Robbie, "but it's not too late. Maybe you're right and we can't stop the asteroid, maybe we can't stop the viruses and half the other horrors. But that doesn't mean the whole world needs to be destroyed. It can still be saved. But to do so, we need to take action now!"

"You're a suberhero, aren't you? Why don't you do somezing?"

"I am! But I need your help."

"Okay, Robbie Cox. We do zis. You tell me your blan. If I like it, we do it. If I don't like it, I feed your young friend here to ze snakes."

Robbie glanced at the copyeditor, who was nervously sipping water and had suddenly turned obnoxiously pale. "Deal," said Robbie, shaking the king's hand.

132.

"Now, get ready! It's time to check back in with the countdown!" said Killian—cartoon Killian.

Flash to the solar system in motion. The sun like a smiley-face sticker, lemon-yellow and happy about everything. Zeroing in on the planet Earth. As if it didn't already look like a sitting duck in the cosmos, there was a bull's-eye on it. A countdown clock appeared at the same time as a ruler stretching from the bull's-eye to a giant asteroid speeding through space.

The countdown clock said: 2 Days, 19 Hours, 47 Minutes, 5 Seconds.

"What are you doing to prepare?" asked Killian joyfully, his animated form floating at the bottom of the screen. "Let's check in with some locals in San Francisco, where the Dudebuddy Festival has everyone taking over the streets in a sea of dancing white bathrobes."

Flash to—

Blackness. Static. A buzzing sound and a crackle. A new image emerging. A grainy image with poor lighting. Not a cartoon...

"May I hab your attention," said an ugly, sour-faced man sitting stiffly on a throne. "Zis is a message for all of you zinking ze Dudebuddy can sabe you. Zinking it's your only hobe, to follow ze Dudebuddy when ze asteroid comes. Or when you are dying of ze plague."

In San Francisco, and everywhere around the world, people stopped what they were doing to crowd around the nearest television to watch this mysterious interruption to the scheduled cartoon show.

The Militant King X readjusted on his throne. At the same time, a green serpent slithered around his body, resting its head on his shoulder. He continued:

"Ze Dudebuddy is ze one causing all of zese catastrophes across ze world. And ze mass media is helbing, turning ze suberheroes against each ozzer. Ze dreams are what Dudebuddy blants in ze minds of ze weak. Ze cry to Liberate Dudebuddy is suicide. It is ze ancient brayer to bring about ze end of ze world. Do not cry Liberate Dudebuddy. Instead, engage in your local bolitical brocess. Write to your leaders in congress, to your bresident. Bay your taxes. Bote for anyzing and eberyzing. It is only zrough zis bolitical brocess zat we can be sabed!"

Then Robbie stepped into the picture, flexing his muscles as he gave a thumbs-up: "I'm Robbie Cox, and I approve this message."

Blackness. Static...

When the screen came up again, it was back to the countdown: 2 Days, 19 Hours, 44 Minutes, 18 Seconds. —17 —16 —15.

133.

Being a superhero had gotten old fast. Killian was already over it. And then suddenly, as if for no reason, he froze in a cold sweat. Wow, he thought, jeez. He remembered something.

It was late one evening at Global Media Headquarters in

London. The normal office workers had gone home for the day. Killian was reclining in a swivel chair, twirling. All around him in the vacant office were screens of endless news broadcasts from around the world. There were so many of them to look at, it was easier just to let his mind wander, rather than to watch any one thing.

But then he had the disconcerting memory. He stopped twirling and just thought about it for a minute. It was about Uncle Jon, something he'd said. "I feel like I've been used." Something like that.

Wow, thought Killian, silently staring past a thousand screens. If being a superhero was nothing but a silly marketing thing, and if he was just being used to be that thing, then what was he doing, really?

Just then the voices in the next room got loud. First Meriwether's voice rose, then Eleanor George's. The next moment they were arguing at the top of their lungs. Killian hopped off the swivel chair and scurried across the room; he peeked around the corner and listened.

Throughout the day, the cartoon broadcasts and even some of the regular news broadcasts had been interrupted by the terrorists Militant King X, Robbie Cox, and the nerdy-looking guy who, it seemed, wrote all the propaganda messages. That's what Eleanor George and Meriwether were so upset about. They couldn't agree on what to do.

Eleanor George said to go and kill them outright. Kill them for everyone to witness on live TV.

Meriwether said doing that was too easy and would likely only further the terrorists' purpose. He proposed doing the less dramatic but strategically sound thing and simply pulling the plug on all mass media communications—even satellite TV and the Internet.

This went back and forth. Killian listened without completely understanding. He wondered what role he might be required to play. Like Uncle Jon, how he might be used.

"Oh good lord," said Eleanor, suddenly turning her attention to the nearest television.

"What's this?" said Meriwether.

Eleanor turned up the volume. It was an Irish station. An overly-excited Irish reporter was shouting the latest news.

"Aw, sure look it!" he shouted. "All this while, the political superpowers the world over couldn't get funding enough for NASA's pea shooter. And now just in time a pot of jewels and a few gold crowns besides have been gifted for the cause. It's the arseways of getting your emergency funds in order, but all we can say is that's this year in politics, ah-hah! Yet why the big news channels are silent on this so far—I'll be damned! Reports just now coming in from Houston say launch time is six hours and counting. Well, looks like we can all go out tonight and drink a pint of Gat and sleep easy, sure look it!"

"Okay," said Meriwether, after a long pause, "new plan."

134.

POLITICAL OP-ED: Now from the pages of your favorite gentlemen's magazine, Hella Naked Ladies Weekly. This being the perfect forum for me to say straight up, real talk: Country Homemakers Magazine can go fuck itself up its frumpy homemaker's ass! Those douches (and I'm so happy I can finally say fuck and douches outright—I don't know why, it just feels so good) have no vision, thin skin, and they don't know politics from a chicken-print quilt duvet. Why else would they have canned me after one innocuous commentary on the big issues facing the world at large?

First a moment of silence for the fact that no other commentators anywhere had faith in our superheroes. Only I did. And now who's got the last laugh. That would be this guy. — Hah!

With plenty of time to spare (about 38 hours), the massive asteroid coming straight for us was shot right out of space. POW! There's this thing in politics that really deserves its own holiday at this point: timing. Starting now, myself and all the good people at Hella Naked Ladies Weekly propose making June 19th the annual Politics Perfect Timing Day in honor of the asteroid being destroyed. Because, come on, was that some perfect timing or what?

To everyone involved in that operation, even the crazy people donating multi-million dollar jewels or whatever, I say great work and good show!

But moving on, let's talk about Cindy Sin Cinnibuns for a moment. Am I right? This week's cover girl, she's not only a babe-quality thing to look at, also she's so pro-politics I'm almost speechless. Right now, she's finishing up her degree in general superhero studies and looking for a career in lingerie and also swimsuit modeling. With academic credentials like she's got, I'd say her ass and perfect-to-look-at breast size is ready for just about anything. What's the next reason the world might end at any moment? If Cindy Cinnibuns has anything to say about it, I'd say we're in good shape!

135.

A rental car pulled up in front of Homunculus Castle. It idled there a moment before the motor shut off. It wasn't anywhere near a parking spot, but it shut off anyway. There was, apparently, no one else around.

Then Sweet Jesus got out. He was wearing sunglasses and a raincoat, looking like a cross between a fashionable bum and an inconspicuous movie star enjoying his golden years. Or just someone lost in the Alps.

He disappeared quickly around a crumbling stone wall. Unlike the average vacationer, Sweet Jesus knew all about secret entrances to the castle. In a matter of minutes, he emerged from a rusted grate in the castle's long-abandoned dungeon.

He dusted himself off and looked around at the skeletons, rats, and moldy darkness. This old world gets me every time, he thought, practically tearing up with comforting nostalgia.

Escaping the dungeon like a gentleman, calmly adjusting the collar of his raincoat, Sweet Jesus climbed a stone staircase up to the main level, where the marble still glistened and the echoes of even the smallest sounds picked up culture and historical nuance with each crevice they bounced off.

"Hello?" called Sweet Jesus. "Anybody here?"

He explored the entire castle. It was all abandoned, just as he had left it, so many months ago. Until finally he came to the top floor of the main edifice, where the war room was housed behind a giant door of hardwood and steal.

The door was shut tight. That's odd, thought Sweet Jesus. In the past, the war room had always been left open for castle tours. He stood there listening, imagining he heard voices inside. Voices arguing about taking over the world. He pressed his ear against the door and listened.

"Stationing troops here and here," said a husky, magisterial voice, "we lay siege on Lutsk, fortifying our stronghold in Lithuania."

"And the Ottomans?" cried a second voice, distraught. "Here...! Here...! We leave ourselves exposed! With forces dispersed in this erratic, haphazard—"

"The Ottomans! You forget! All this time, Bohemia has been quietly positioning its forces along the border, ready to..."

Sweet Jesus pushed on the door. It opened without a sound. Inside, the room was aglow with sunlight streaming in from massive, cathedral-like windows. In the center of the room, two men in kingly robes were leaning over a detailed map of sixteenth century Europe.

"Well!" one of them exclaimed, as if taking this interruption as a personal insult.

"Hello?" said the other, as if he'd anticipated this all along and was strangely self-conscious about it.

"Good day," said Sweet Jesus. "You must be Charlie and Al, the medieval kings." He walked forward, extending his hand in greeting. "Welcome!" he said. "I wasn't sure you'd come. I must say, I had almost given up hope!"

"We got lost," said Al, giving a handshake.

"That's what happens," said Charlie, irritably, "when you're dragged from retirement, a few centuries out of context."

"Although," Al added, "time seems to be off. It's hard to tell whether a day has passed or a decade since we got back."

"I summoned you here," said Sweet Jesus, "due to urgent necessity, I assure you." His mind flashed back to the moment in the bikini rodeo bar when he'd read the incantation on a drunken whim.

"Don't worry," said Charlie, "we sent our crowns to save the world from the asteroid."

"We didn't even know about it until when we arrived at the castle," Al explained, pointing at the large television on the far wall. "When we learned about it, we figured that's why we must have been summoned back. To do something."

"I know," said Sweet Jesus. "As soon as I heard that NASA had received funding through jewels and gold crowns, I knew you had arrived. I came here right after I heard the news."

"Good," said Charlie. "So we did fulfill our purpose sending in our crowns like that."

"It was close," said Al. "We almost used our crowns to build a new mote."

"True," said Charlie, nodding his head in grave sincerity. "The castle is in dire need of a mote. If we are to begin our campaign to conquer all the miserable governments of the pagan nations, we must begin by fortifying our castle with a mote."

"But like I told Charlie," Al interjected, "what good is having a mote if the whole castle along with the entirety of Europe is destroyed by a falling demon star?"

"Ah, ha!" Sweet Jesus cried happily. "And that's precisely why I summoned the two most industrious kings of medieval Europe. Only sovereign monarchs can effectuate pragmatic action in a time of crisis. All other politicians are stalemated by constituents and media contracts—especially when it counts."

"So, it is finished, right?" Charlie asked.

"Yes," said Sweet Jesus. "At least in terms of the asteroid. It has been destroyed."

"Great! Then we can finally get to work doing something

productive. Come over here a moment, my good sir. Take a look." Charlie spread out his arms over the table, indicating the ancient map of Europe. "Here we have Lithuania; and extending all the way from here...to here, we have the Ottoman Empire. We can assume Bohemia is ours, and that Poland is soon to fall. We have troops here, here, and here."

"I don't mean to interrupt," said Sweet Jesus. "But I'm afraid your map is several hundred years out of date. These borders are entirely wrong. The Ottoman Empire was destroyed long ago."

Charlie folded his arms, scratched his chin, thinking this over. "Yes, I was concerned about that. Al, didn't I tell you?! We need a new map!"

"And a mote," said Al.

"Yes," said Charlie, nodding solemnly. "We do still need a mote."

136.

"All set, kid?" Meriwether asked, giving a thumbs-up.

Killian was on next. It was the last broadcast he'd ever have to do. Following a pre-recorded announcement by Eleanor George, Killian would be live. With his youth and charm, he'd make the message appeal to the masses. His broadcast would instantaneously be transcribed into cartoon form, which is, after all, the ideal medium for politics.

Cartoons are mythic but relatable. They don't take themselves too seriously. No one wants a myth that's self-absorbed. Also cartoons are fast and entertaining. Here's everything you need to know in five seconds. That's right! It's everything you need to know and isn't it all so hilarious?!

"All set," said Killian.

This was Meriwether's plan. It was simple yet brilliant. First, Eleanor George would explain away Robbie Cox and Militant King X with her message from behind the scenes, from the position of undeniable respectability. She would state the obvious. Robbie Cox and Militant King X are terrorists. Do not listen to them. They don't want what's best for you. They want what terrorists want. Which is, bad things. They want bad things to happen to you.

As a casual viewer, it would be impossible to not think: Well, obviously!

Then Killian would come on. He'd say: Guess what! Playing your part in defeating the terrorists is so easy! All you have to do is this! Just go outside and stand on the street corner. Just go out there right now and chant: Liberate Dudebuddy! Can you do that? You do want to stamp out terrorism, don't you? Okay! Then let's go! Chant with me! Liberate Dudebuddy! Liberate Dudebuddy! Liberate Dudebuddy! Yeah! he'd say. Yeah! That's it!

137.

It was a big moment and everyone knew it. When Eleanor George spoke, it was something. It could mean the debut of a new cartoon show. Or a declaration of world peace. Something big.

What she said was, Don't listen to terrorists.

And all the sick, plague-ridden, and dying peoples the world over listened enthralled and thought, Well, obviously!

Then the screen flashed at the bottom that this was LIVE. And it was the new superhero Killian Gladstone for everyone to listen to next.

He said, as his politician's smile fled his cartoon face, Okay, forget everything you were just told. Eleanor George is a liar and all the stuff Robbie Cox and Militant King X have been saying is true. Dudebuddy is behind all the recent disasters happening. And the mass media, which Eleanor George controls, knows it.

Whatever you do, he said, don't say Liberate Dudebuddy out loud. It will only help cause more terrible disasters.

And he went on, hurrying, talking as fast as he could, Anyway, if you're watching this and you don't want the world to end, and especially if you're sick and dying, come to Homunculus Castle right away. That's the only safe place. It's the most political place on the planet—the complete opposite of, you know, Arkansas—and you'll be safe there. Also, there you'll find the cure to the plague. Come to Homunculus Castle if you want to live! And remember that whatever you do, don't say Liberate Dudebud—

The screen went dark. It went dark and then everything went to static. Just like that. And it didn't come back.

138.

Sweet Jesus was idling in a getaway car outside Global Media Headquarters, expecting Killian to appear at any moment. There was no plan. There was only this message from Killian, sent to Homunculus Castle a few days ago, saying, "Sweet Jesus, meet me outside GMH" with the date, the time, and signed "Kill."

"I could be entirely out of line," said Sweet Jesus, talking to himself as he tapped on the getaway car's steering wheel, "but by God things do not feel right." A moment later he said, "Oh, hang it all!" and got out of the car.

Under his three-piece suit, which he removed in broad daylight without a care, he wore his classic superhero attire.

"I've scaled you before," he said to the giant skyscraper, "and I can scale you again."

And so he began his ascent, one hand over the other, aiming straight for Eleanor George's penthouse.

He was about two stories up when someone called his name. He looked down, expecting to see a loyal fan, or perhaps a newspaper reporter wanting an interview. But it was Killian, standing just outside the main entrance, waiving up at him.

"Come on!" Killian hollered. "We have to go!"

139.

Half a universe away in the Interstellar Space Station, Eleanor George, wearing her sexy Alalia costume, was quietly sobbing at the control board. The space station was passing into a new dimension. Everything was distorted; nothing was familiar. It might have been a million years that passed by; it might have been two seconds.

"What happened?" Alalia asked, between sobs.

"I..." said Meriwether, vaguely watching the screen that was before him. "I don't know."

The screen showed—in "real" time—a recording of some sort. It was from the perspective, apparently, of a security camera. There was a guy standing behind a camera. The guy said something like, "I'm not sure if that's what you were supposed to say."

Then some other guy came into the picture. A generic television-crew-member type of guy. He said: "I just pulled the plug on it because I thought... You know, it just seemed... Sorry," he said, looking at his feet.

"It's okay," said the guy who was clearly the only superhero in the room—Killian. "But I guess I should probably get going now."

"Sure. Okay," said the guy behind the camera.

But then one of the crew guys stopped Killian. "Hey, is it true what you just said? I mean, about having the cure? My girl has the plague, and everything, that's all. I was just wondering, if, um..."

"Yeah, it's true," said Killian. "Just come on down to Homunculus Castle. There's plenty of cure for everybody."

"Psh," said Meriwether to himself. "Politics."

"I hate...I hate politics," Alalia sobbed. "I just don't get it. I just...I just..."

"God, me neither," said Meriwether, now pouring himself a tropical cocktail.

"I mean...uh, uh..." Alalia gasped. "We're the good guys, right?!"

"Mm, hm," said Meriwether. "Yeah, we're on the side of everything that's good and amazing. Happiness, easy-breezy living. No fighting, misunderstandings, or war..."

"I don't get it," said Alalia, drying her eyes as they pulled the space station into the solar system of Dudebuddy Nation. "I just don't."

140.

Charlie and Al stood in the lookout tower at Homunculus Castle holding swords and binoculars. The sun was just coming up over the jagged mountain peaks. The entire world, it seemed, was as peaceful as though it had been painted, framed, hung up, and was collecting dust on the wall of a spiritual guru's waiting room—or someplace serene and innocuous like that. Charlie and Al were apparently enjoying it well enough. Although Al couldn't help griping about having gotten out of bed so early.

"Shut up!" said Charlie, suddenly. "You see that?"

"Where?"

They both peered through binoculars down into the perilous ravines.

"There," said Charlie.

"I'm not registering," said Al.

"Well," Charlie grabbed his royal companion by the neck and tilted his head down and to the left, "try off that way—see?"

"Ah. Hm... Oh. Oh!"

"You see?"

"A procession!" cried Al, finally seeing the long line of cars winding along a steep hillside far below.

"At last," Charlie said, raising his sword high into the air, "our army has arrived!"

141.

Sweet Jesus in his getaway car was the first to pull up in front of Homunculus Castle. He and Killian quickly rushed inside and made arraignments to begin procuring the antidote hidden in Killian's blood. A team of medical professionals, including a number of anti-plague specialists, would be arriving shortly.

The television crew guys from Global Media Headquarters arrived next. They had stopped along the way to pick up all their sick friends and relatives. Knocking on the castle door, they were welcomed by Sweet Jesus, who led them to the ancient theater where the world leaders' conference was held.

Before long, the ancient theater was overflowing with the sick, plague-ridden masses. And still people from all over the world continued to flood into the castle. At one point, word spread that Robbie Cox, Militant King X, and the infamous copyeditor had arrived. Their presence caused such a stir that even the two monarchs, who had locked themselves in the war room, heard the news.

"Bring them in!" said Charlie to Sweet Jesus, who had assumed his old position as castle caretaker.

"Righto," said Sweet Jesus.

That afternoon, the two monarchs made their first strategic military decision, declaring Robbie Cox and Militant King X to be commanding generals in the new royal army.

"Zat sounds like just like my bag of snakes!" King X hissed, respectfully bowing to the monarch.

"And there's no election?" Robbie asked, skeptically. "We just get the job—just like that?"

"Of course zere's no election," said King X. "Zese two are sobereigns. Zey do not know ze meaning of election!"

"And you," said Charlie, pointing a gold scepter at the copyeditor, "you will be the new royal scribe."

"Yes, your highness," said the new scribe, bowing awkwardly as his eyes wandered suspiciously over the various maps and notes scrawled all over the walls of the medieval war room.

142.

This chapter was supposed to be about the end of the world. Except, it's now an act of treason to even mention the possibility of the world ending. So, even if the world has ended, you won't be hearing about it from me.

Oh, hey, it's the royal scribe here. Still getting used to the new job title. Not to mention the ridiculous outfit that comes with it. The new employers, apparently, are quite serious about their thing for medieval fashion. Dress codes to me just seem old fashioned. But who am I to complain?

My job is to rewrite history. So you know there's a lot to do. Also when it comes to reporting on the daily news, you can never be too careful what you say. Can't ever make the royalty look bad. That's rule number one. Also the kingdom is always expanding in wealth, happiness, and moral correctness—making sure everyone knows that is rule number two.

At the moment, the main thing is reporting on the crusades. That's what we're calling it. The crusades. Which is the military operation to take back all territories infested with the bathrobed people with the fake beards. Robbie Cox and Militant King X are leading the charge. Anyone caught wearing a white bathrobe and/or a fake beard is captured and turned into a serf.

In other news, I now have my own copyeditor, of sorts. He's a former political op-ed writer of some racy gentlemen's magazine. His opinions are off-base about ninety percent of the time, but so far that doesn't seem to interfere with his ability to skew history and compose a thoughtful sentence every now and then.

143.

HOMUNCULUS GAZZETE: Mass media is dead! Cartoons are dead! Even Hella Naked Ladies, that fine publication of prurient interests and saucy political commentary, has come to an end! But, folks, we're still here. You and me. The plague couldn't get us and neither could those alien creeps trying to suck our brains out with their weirdo anarchism.

Politics for the win! That's what I'm saying! Specifically, I'm talking about monarchy, the only system that does the trick. Now anyone can be a superhero. All you've got to do is get into the royal family. Or get knighted. To tell the truth, I'm not sure how many ways there are to become a superhero in a sovereign state. I'd say, just be a loyal subject to the throne and you'll be pointed in the right direction!

Now if we could only find Killian Gladstone. First he saves the planet from apparently every nasty thing ever with his blood, then he vanishes. The kings are offering a small fief for anyone with news leading to the recovery of the young champion. What's a fief? I'm not entirely sure, to be frank. You'll have to look it up yourself. But I understand there might be a few cows thrown into the mix as, I've been told, fiefs can get awfully lonely at times without the proper livestock.

144.

Interview with a common member of serfdom, formerly a Caucasian landowner, pt. 10: "Starting a Revolution" (WARNING: This interview series is unedited. When encountering agricultural laborers in the feudal system, bear in mind that lack of breeding often manifests in the most ungodly of mannerisms. The proper response to a peasant's attempt at expressing an opinion is, of course, to simply chortle to oneself and move along.)

INTERVIEWER: Nowhere to go but up. Must feel liberating.

COMMON SERF: They took my house, took my land, even took away my bathrobe. That was all I had left!

I: These are difficult times. Everyone must make some sacrifice. Or perhaps you've found a meaning in your loss of possessions? Perhaps you feel you're now a wiser, more enriched person in your humble state?

CS: I say, death to the nobility! Off with their fat heads!

I: So you've taken quickly to the rebellious stereotype associated with your lowly existence. A question for you.

CS: Whatever. Make it good!

I: Let's say you topple the nobility and overthrow the kings. What next? What sort of government would you put up in its place?

CS: Easy. One with no taxes, one where there's no voting except as a form of punishment, one where I've got a big mansion and a plot of land I can do whatever the hell I want with, one where I can say anything and nobody can tell me what to do, and one where I'm rich by default and working is optional.

I: Would everybody be able to live like that, or just you?

CS: Ask a hundred people what they want in a government, they'll all tell you something different. I'm just speaking for myself. If someone likes being a goddamn serf in a goddamn fief, let 'em!

I: So, in this political iteration, you'd prefer to be king?

CS: Just let me out of the whole mess! I can't take it anymore! Just give me a huge house with no taxes and leave me the hell alone!

I: If the world were to end at any moment—

CS: Let it!

politicians are superheroes

Peter Clarke holds a BA in psychology and a JD in intellectual property law. His short fiction has appeared widely in literary journals including 3AM Magazine, Curbside Splendor, and Hobart. He's an assistant editor for Fifth Wednesday Journal and founding editor of Jokes Review. Native to Port Angeles, Washington, he currently lives in Oakland, California.

www.petermclarke.com

323 East Avenue
Lockport, NY 14094
www.pskisporch.com

Pski's Porch Publishing was formed July 2012, to make
books for people who like people who like books.
We hope we have some small successes.
www.pskisporch.com.